THE ZARTAR]
by Ana F

Revie

This is a truly delightful book focussed mainly at 7-12 year olds although it has a far wider appeal for older ages, and really anyone who loves fantasy and adventure... First print run has been an immediate sell out.
Amazon.co.uk

A modern twist on the classic fantasy theme of good versus evil – it was great and gripped me to the end. Roll on Book 2.
Best Magazine

It has all the makings of a runaway success.
Stuart Webb, Book & Magazine Collector

It takes a strong creative adult to successfully transport young readers into a world of make believe and author Ana Fischel is definitely one such talented person.
Hi! Society Magazine

Sure to be a classic children's book.
Lincolnshire Today

Ana Fischel´s new book... is set to be one of the literary sensations of the year.
Thurrock Gazette

... the world she has created is particularly original and stylish. Her characters boast intensely expressive faces and don intricate and colourful costumes.
Estepona Magazine

... it is pleasing to see the arrival of a thoughtful and inspiring new storybook aimed at the wizard weary young reader... her story is equally as enticing and seductive as the works of Miss Rowling. The characters are wonderfully and intimately portrayed... Aided by the stunning illustrations... an utterly absorbing and tantalising experience for young readers and their parents... the book has a wonderful pace and energy to it.

Vivid December 2004

... the story is easy to follow, yet rich with adventure, humour and the style of imaginative story-telling that lures them into an escapist world they will not want to leave...

Fujairah Observer December 2004

... the writings and illustrations are captivating enough to make us patiently await the following episodes of this marvellous epic tale into a mysterious and magical world.

Rugrats Magazine January 2005

The Zartarbia Tales is for anyone who loves fantasy and adventure. There is also a cast of intriguing and unusual characters who can keep you glued to the adventure... It is a fantasy with lots of action... I liked the story as it is very imaginative. I would recommend this book to boys and girls... The pace of the book is quite fast and the reader will always be interested... this book is a real page turner... This is one book I would recommend to our book club...

The Zartarbia Tales was the chosen Winner out of pop star Darius "Live Twice" and the video game Spongebob Square Pants; CBBC Television Book Xchange

The Zartarbia Tales

BOOK 2

Isabella Zophie and The Hotel Gastronomic

**Illustrated and written
by Ana Fischel**

ISBN 1-905203-16-0

First published in Great Britain in 2005 by
Pen Press Publishers Ltd
39 Chesham Rd
Brighton BN2 1NB

For further information visit www.zartarbia.com
or www.penpress.net

The Zartarbia Tales

BOOK 2

Isabella Zophie and The Hotel Gastronomic

The Zartarbia Tales support ChildLine, the children's charity which provides a 24-hour telephone helpline for any child with any problem. Children can call free on 0800 1111 from any phone, at any time. ChildLine depends on donations and always needs funds to pay for the children's calls and to train volunteer counsellors.

Donations can be sent to ChildLine (Zartarbia partnership), Freepost NATN1111, London E1 6BR, with cheques made payable to ChildLine. More information about ChildLine, including how to become a volunteer counsellor, can be found at www.childline.org.uk

"The Zartarbia Tales create a magical world of fantasy that children can escape into, but at the same time help children to navigate some of the aspects of life that are challenging, scary or unpleasant. That mirrors what we do at ChildLine, supporting children to find ways through their problems and giving them hope and emotional resilience, which is why we're delighted to be working in partnership with The Zartarbia Tales."

Natasha Finlayson, Director of Communications and Policy at ChildLine

Supporting

ChildLine

0800 1111

Reg'd charity no.1003758

"The Zartarbia Tales addresses difficult and controversial issues that children and young people are trying to grapple with in a sensitive and engaging way. Having ChildLine on board can only strengthen the impact of her books."

Mary O'Hara, Reporter The Guardian

Three Heroines
Chloe✝Caoimhe✝Lauren

Dedicated to….

Gustav
An incredible husband and a patient manager
For your enduring love, support and tolerating my cantankerous
ways
You are the other half that makes me whole, crazy and sane

Isabella and Lujzka
You have no idea of the happiness you bring to us
Enjoy your childhoods as long as you can
I hope that your children will enjoy these books as much as I have
writing them

Isaac
My adorable nephew and godson

To all grandparents who take the time to nurture their
grandchildren's imagination but in particular:
Sophie and Bruno, Jane and Patrick and Rowena and William

My Great Aunty Cis and her school Raventhorpe
You inspired this story
My time with you was always seeped in magic
I miss you and that twinkle in your eyes

Pen Press Publishing
Thank you for all your hard work.
We raise a glass to all of you!

Jacqui MacCarthy at D'Image Ltd
"Thank you for being not only a brilliant publicist,
but also a good friend."

And last but not least to three special heroines
Chloe, Caoimhe and Lauren

ILLUSTRATIONS LISTING:
PROLOGUE
Three Heroines – Agent Chloe, Lauren and Caoimhe

EPILOGUE

NOTES TO THE READER

COMPETITION

CHAPTER LISTING:
PROLOGUE

Prologue

Charles Mortensen sat by the fire, sucking on his pipe and pondering the sheaf of parchments that lay on his lap. He looked up, frowning, as his wife Beatrice entered his study and exhaled a plume of smoke.

"I'm working. I thought I told you I didn't want to be disturbed!" he said sharply returning to his papers.

"I thought you might like some hot chocolate. I've just made some," she said quietly setting down a tray on a table next to him. "What are you doing my dear?"

"It's just a project I've been working on. Nothing that would interest you."

Beatrice bit her lip, wondering why her husband had become so secretive recently. She picked up a poker and started to stoke the fire. Outside, daggers of rain slashed at the window and a ferocious wind tore through the night.

"I wish this weather would improve," remarked Beatrice, as she peered out through the curtains. "It's been like this for weeks."

"Um," he said not really listening to her. It had been several months since that strange evening when an old merchant had slipped the documents into his coat pocket along with an ancient

locket. Though he specialised in translating obsolete languages and obscure dialects, these inscriptions were proving difficult.

He picked up a magnifying glass, staring intently at the carefully drawn characters. Part of him wanted to dismiss the merchant's story of another world as just the ranting of a madman, but there was something that niggled inside him; a subconscious voice that said, 'what if he was telling the truth...'

Professor Mortensen was a practical man, not given to flights of fantasy, but there was something within the inscriptions, some ancient code that fascinated him. From what he had managed to decipher so far, he had worked out that parts of the manuscript originated from an early Peruvian dialect but part also seemed embedded in some type of ritualistic magic. He picked up a dusty leather bound book and carefully leafed through its yellow pages. He had searched for a mention of Zartarbia amongst his vast library of reference books but there had been nothing. He seemed to draw a blank everywhere he looked. He let out a sigh, feeling most agitated.

"Are you going to be much longer my dear?" enquired his wife. "You've been working so hard lately. Maybe an early night is what you need."

"I'm fine," he said crossly, scribbling something down in a notebook.

"Really, Charles, I don't know what's got into you recently. Ever since that night... well, I'm sure you would tell me if something was wrong... it's just that you have not been yourself since," said Beatrice, looking hurt.

"There's nothing wrong! How many times do I have to tell you!" he snapped.

She walked slowly over to his desk and picked up the locket, "This looks expensive. I thought you had bought it as a

Christmas present for me, but after Christmas Day came and went...well it's obviously for somebody else. Who is it?" she said, trying to remain composed. "It's clear that you have no interest in me anymore but I thought you would have the decency to at least be discreet with gifts for another woman."

"What are you talking about?" he said brusquely.

"This! This is what I'm talking about!" she said throwing the necklace onto her husband's lap. "In all the years we have been married you have never bought me anything as valuable as this. I thought... well, I came across it when I was organising your correspondence a few weeks ago... what else should I think!"

Beatrice turned her back on him sobbing. "Well clearly you are in no mood for conversation tonight, so I shall retire."

He looked up at her, his expression softening. "Beatrice, wait! It's not what you think!"

"I said to myself, I've been a good wife, a good mother... why would you do this to me?" she said wiping a tear from her eye.

"Beatrice, stop being so foolish," he said standing up and cupping her face in his hands. "There is no other woman. There's just you."

"Then why have you been so withdrawn? You barely say two words to me!"

"I'm sorry. I didn't mean to be testy with you. Look it's an artefact I am studying – it's not for anybody... in fact, it's not mine to give..." he said smiling gently. "I love you, you know that don't you my dear? You and Auriel are the most precious things in my life. It's just that when I'm working, I get so involved."

He kissed her on the forehead. "I'm sorry if I have distressed you. Forgive me? Let us go to bed now. It's late, and we're *both tired," he said, leading his wife upstairs.*

Outside on the street, a figure stood in the shadows watching the house. He bided his time, finishing his cigarette, before creeping towards the house and sliding a knife under the windowsill.

"Damn!" he muttered under his breath as the wooden frame refused to budge.

He didn't dare smash the glass but equally he didn't want to return to his boss empty handed. He could see a glimmer of the locket, reflected in the dying embers of the fire. And then a thought came to him...

Chapter One
THE ARRIVAL OF ESPECTRO UNDERWELT

The heavy ominous roll of drums signalled the approach of Espectro Underwelt - King of Undead Souls and the most demonic member of The Syndicate.

He flicked back the curtain of his carriage, looking indifferently at the rain-saturated clouds that encompassed the horizon. He was flanked by an army of warriors, bodyguards and fearsome creatures.

The Snarlton (a particularly vicious type of monster) that was harnessed to the front of his vehicle roared as the driver hit it again with a spiked whip. The creature was hideous beyond comprehension. It had three rows of teeth which were sharper than a shark's and that dripped with blood from its last meal. It could also spit venom that was so deadly it could kill a man a mile away if he was to be struck by its saliva. These monsters were trained from birth to kill. It was all they knew, brutality and death, and these characteristics were certainly in abundance in the world Espectro ruled. He was a man consumed by evil and hatred, whose only pleasure was derived from the casual violence and misery he inflicted on other people. Torture and terror were the corner stones behind his dictatorship and, to emphasis this point, he had the souls of his victims tattooed onto his body. As you can imagine, being such a bloody and prolific murderer there was little of his flesh that was not inscribed. His entire body was a huge graveyard, each tattoo like a tombstone. Indeed Espectro Underwelt embodied every fear that a reasonable person might feel, and to his enemies, the mere mention of his name was enough to give a grown adult nightmares for years.

As they drew nearer to Segregaria, the sky suddenly blackened as a huge formation of ravens flew across, blocking out the receding daylight.

"Give me a drink," he shouted up to a servant that was perched on the carriage roof. The servant quickly poured some wine into a skull and handed it to him. Espectro grunted and smiled as he drank, the boy's speed of service had certainly improved since he had witnessed what had happened to his predecessor! He finished his drink and threw the skull out of the window where it was crushed under the intimidating feet of his entourage.

Meanwhile…

Security was extremely tight at the palatial castle where Oro Cazador resided. Cameras swivelled this way and that, scanning the vast acres of swamp that surrounded the castle. It was a formidable place with huge metal doors and hundreds of tiny windows made from bullet-proof glass. All those who entered or left had to pass through a sophisticated scanning device that checked the barcode implants everyone in the lands of Glutonious and Segregaria was forced to have.

Glace Cazador, Oro's sister, had personally overseen the security arrangements for The Syndicate summit. She was a tall and slender woman who, from a distance, might be mistaken as looking fragile. It was not until you got closer that you realized

Espectro Underverde visiting Segregaria

nothing could be further from the truth. Her face was pinched and steely, her eyes cold and hooded, almost reptilian. Her skin was a pale blue and so thin that you could see the veins faintly beneath it. When she stood still she looked as if she were dead. She wore her raven black hair pinned up, fashioned into two pointed cones that were encased with a metallic netting. She was waiting by the entrance when Espectro Underwelt arrived. One of the guards opened the carriage door for him and the cloaked figure of Espectro flowed out, his powerful presence making even Glace feel uneasy.

"Welcome Mr Underwelt. Come this way please." She led him over to the scanner system. "If you could leave any weapons here and, I apologise, but your associates will have to remain in the perimeter areas. My brother was very clear that only Syndicate members be present at the meeting. I shall arrange for them to be taken to the staff quarters where refreshments have been prepared for them."

"You can tell your brother that he gets more paranoid every time I see him!" Espectro snapped, but none the less nodded at his men to wait for him there.

"He's just cautious…especially after Sectica…well, her unfortunate death. One can't be too careful in uncertain times such as these. Any one of us could be next."

"Nonsense…the woman was so conceited it was only a matter of time," growled Espectro. "She got above herself in thinking that nobody could get to her. You wouldn't find that happening in my kingdom."

"Anyway you are a little early Mr Underwelt - the rest of the members have not arrived yet. Permit me to accompany you to the Inner Sanctum where there will be servants at your disposal to make your visit as comfortable as possible."

Glace's expression gave nothing away as she led him along a

vast and elaborate corridor. The wallpaper was gold leaf, edged by skirting boards that were studded with pearls and opals. Every few paces stood heavily armed soldiers who clicked their heels to attention as Glace passed them.

Finally they arrived at a great circular hallway. It was an ostentatious affair, decorated with the most expensive fabrics and rarest of treasures. It was a well known fact that Oro had an all-consuming obsession with collecting extraordinary things - whether they were inanimate or breathing.

Glace snapped her fingers at a nearby fireplace and suddenly crackling flames sprang up from the hearth. Espectro went over to the fire to warm himself, standing on a rug that started to fidget and move. It clearly startled him and he jumped back, kicking it hard with a metal capped boot. "What the hell is going on?!!"

Glace quickly clapped her hands at it and the rug rolled itself up. "Apologies Mr Underwelt. It is a flying carpet…one of my brother's latest acquisitions. It is young and is still in the process of being house trained."

"I don't appreciate being made a fool of!" he bellowed.

"I can assure you that was not my intention," said Glace evenly. "Now if you will excuse me I need to check to see if any of the other members have arrived. If you need anything, just press this button."

Espectro watched as the woman glided out of the room, thinking to himself that she was one of the most unattractive females he had ever seen. He turned on the heel of his boot and stood for a moment studying the vast hall in which he stood. Fine paintings hung from the walls; display cabinets were stuffed full of fans that belonged to film stars and storms that had been collected from the top of the highest mountains. There was an eyelash plucked from an ancient princess that sat next to a seagull's song trapped in a tiny glass phial. There were slippers made from the softest clouds and a necklace dripping with unshed tears. Above the fireplace hung two dragon's teeth the length of a man's arm. Espectro also noticed a rather forlorn-looking cherub with curls so matted that it looked as if his head had grown claws. He was sitting back against his tiny folded wings in a large cage suspended over a balcony. Nearby a young mermaid slept in a tank, her floating hair entwined with sea anemones. Shooting stars and fireflies flew overhead. Opposite the fireplace was a glass fountain that spouted rainbows and next to that high up on a shelf was a bottle containing a rather disgruntled looking genie.

One of Oro's butlers entered, bringing a tray of refreshments for Espectro. He set it down, presenting a variety of delicacies and a flagon of wine.

"Sir…Chef has prepared some refreshments for you," he announced.

"What is this muck?" shouted Espectro, picking up a quail's leg and hurling it across the room.

"Nouvelle cuisine Sir, the best, or so I've been reliably informed by chef. Apparently it's all the rage," replied the butler politely. "But if it is not to Sir's satisfaction, I can arrange something else."

"Get me some proper grub," snarled Espectro, "and be quick about it!"

"Certainly Sir," said the man bowing deeply. "Will there be anything else, Sir?"

"Just make sure somebody informs me the moment the rest of The Syndicate has arrived!" Espectro said rudely.

Chapter Two
THE SYNDICATE SUMMIT

Oro Cazador, meanwhile, was sitting at his desk, darkly contemplating the various possible outcomes of the summit. He had to ensure that The Syndicate worked together this time. For the moment, he needed his fellow colleagues if they were to defeat the FADF.

Oro was an imposing man, unattractive and grossly overweight yet strangely debonair. His large, portly body was due to a lifetime of overindulgence (for Oro was a man that denied himself nothing and his appetite was insatiable). He didn't think twice about eating in one sitting the same amount of food a normal person would eat in a week! His favourite meal was game pie to start with, followed by a whole cow (spit roasted minus the head, hooves and tail) served with a huge dish of fried potatoes, followed by chocolate cake smothered with double cream and finished off with an enormous selection of cheese and biscuits. This he would wash down with several gallons of rich red wine and a bottle of the finest port. As we all know, this was not the healthiest of diets but none of the doctors that attended upon Oro Cazador dared say a word about his lifestyle, even though he was so obese that he found it difficult to dress himself.

His face was round with flabby jowls of flesh hanging either side and a wet spongy mouth that was framed with a spiky moustache. Oro's most distinguishing feature was his grotesque glass eye that was squashed in between rolls of slack skin. This glass eye acted like a scanner as Oro trusted no one. It was larger than the average size of an eye , which made his other one appear tiny and piggy looking. In contrast to his ugliness, Oro had extremely good taste and always had to have the best of everything. He was a man of top tailors and exclusive eau de colognes. His wealth was legend, as was his ability to spend it. He could be immensely charming when he deemed it necessary, and many a woman had fallen for this fake demeanour, only to regret it at a later date (for if truth be known Oro hated all women with the exception of one - his daughter, Lily Rose).

He turned as his sister entered, his glass eye swivelling in its socket. "Well?"

"They are all here except for Mr Fortuno. Shall I show them in now or do you want to wait for him?"

Oro nodded brusquely. "Show them in. That imbecile Devin is always late."

He pushed himself up from the desk and walked over to the large conference table to greet each of The Syndicate members as they slowly filed in.

"Welcome. I thank you for attending this summit today," said Oro. extending a spade-like hand to each of them.

"Espectro, I apologise to have kept you waiting. I trust the journey did not incommode you too much?" he said shaking the other man's hand firmly (for whilst there was little trust within the Syndicate, Oro and Espectro were close allies).

"The journey was crap and you need to fire your chef!" growled Espectro.

"I see I find you in your normal good humour comrade," said Oro amiably, ignoring Espectro's complaints.

Next was Tempest Pestilencia, a vicious pirate who evolved from the sin of Envy. "It has been a while Mr Cazador," he said. "Let's hope today's meeting will be beneficial to all of us."

Oro smiled and gestured for him to be seated.

"My dear Flores, you look as radiant as ever," he said kissing her hand. (Flores Abunda was derived from the sin of Lust, whose powers of seduction meant she could control the heart of any man with the exception of the Syndicate).

"Save it darling," she purred. "I'm only interested in one thing and that's what you can do for me."

"You mean, what we can do for each other my dear," replied Oro, smiling coldly.

"We'll see," said Flores shaking her long black hair as she glided past him. Fingimiento followed, always a disturbing presence with his intimidating masks. Nobody knew what he actually looked like underneath his customary disguises.

"Cazador, I trust this meeting will not be a waste of my time," he lisped.

"None of us want to waste our time," said Oro sharply. "Let's not get off on the wrong foot. After all, we all want what is best for the Syndicate, don't we? Now please be seated."

Oro walked to the head of the table and placed his hands squarely either side of himself.

"Right! Obviously you all know why I have called for this meeting," Oro began, without waiting for any acknowledgement. "The Federation Against Dark Forces are once more gaining strength and have over half of the Zartarbian territories under their protection after Sectica's demise. Now that we are all gathered together, we need to address the problem of the FADF. Our armies have been weakened after our last battle to regain control of Tivany and Narcissimal. We have all suffered many losses, this is costing us dearly not just in terms of soldiers, after all they are replaceable, but in terms of finance…this is costing each of us a lot of money! We must strike back! We must strike at the core of the FADF, at the heart of their headquarters!" he shouted banging his fist on the table.

"That's easier said than done!" snarled Espectro. "The security system is impenetrable, it's not as if we haven't tried before….even with our combined talents it would be impossible as things stand at the moment!"

"Their undercover agents are everywhere and they have the support of the people even in our own colonies. They would make traitors of our own servants and soldiers!" said Fingimiento from behind his mask.

"Then they must be rooted out," said Glace quietly. "They must be made examples of, them and their families."

"We do not need to encourage our own people to rise against us," interjected Flores.

"Fear is the only form of control," countered Glace.

"Agreed," said Espectro. "Terror is the only way to strike at the heart of communities."

At that precise moment, Devin Fortuno sauntered into the room. As usual, and much to the annoyance of the other Syndicate members, he did not even apologise for his late appearance.

"Well here we are again!" he said sarcastically. "Dear friends reunited."

"You are late Mr Fortuno," said Oro, his flaccid face struggling between gravity and a scowl.

Devin walked over to the only remaining spare chair and plonked himself into it, swinging his feet onto the table. "Well I'm here now. So what did I miss?"

"Everybody else managed to be here on time. Do not presume to think that your time is more important than ours - now get your boots off my table!"

"Suit yourself," replied Fortuno flippantly. "I'm just here for the side show."

"I don't know why you bothered summoning him here at all – we all know he's a waste of space!" grunted Espectro.

"He is still a Syndicate member and as such his opinion must be taken into account. Anyway the reason I asked you all to come today is that I have a proposition..." said Oro pressing a button. A large map levitated from inside the table which showed all the Zartarbian territories as they moved, changing shape and location, shrinking and expanding.

"These are the weakest countries," said Oro pointing a walking stick at the map. "Parisio, Electrodia and Topsy Turney."

"So what?" said Flores. "They are still under the protection of the FADF, and to wage wars in these places would cost us even more casualties."

"Not war as we have done before," said Oro carefully.

"Well what then?" asked Fingimiento.

"We plant specially trained spies, preferably Transcenders, into these areas and we co-ordinate a series of terrorist attacks on these innocent communities so that the FADF will disperse agents to these territories. We will continue these isolated attacks in other areas, naturally distancing ourselves from the actual events, and the FADF will concentrate on capturing the culprits. They will be thrown off balance, their attention diverted."

"But how does this help us to gain control of the whole of Zartarbia?" asked Fingimiento.

"I am getting to that...whilst they are occupied trying to prevent further attacks, we shall be preparing our armies to storm Securical."

"I like it," smiled Espectro. "We create maximum fear with minimum risk to our assets. Once Securical has been conquered, the rest of Zartarbia will be relatively easy to take."

"Transcenders are notoriously tricky," said Devin.

"Their loyalties can be bought at the right price…and besides it is the easiest way to infiltrate these communities," interjected Fingimiento. "It will, however, take time and careful planning."

"Who will co-ordinate these attacks, and train the terrorists?" asked Tempest.

"I propose my head of security Betrug Espion. He is, after all, a Transcender himself…" said Oro.

"But he is under your control and therefore any terrorist armies that he trained would have alliance with you, rather than the rest of us," said Fingimiento.

"What about each of us selecting one of our own to train the Transcenders with Mr Espion – that would be fairer," said Flores.

"It would be havoc," said Espectro dismissively. "No, I agree with Oro. There needs to be a master commander for an operation of this scale to work. We just need to come up with a solution we are all happy with. I propose my commander-in-chief as he has the appetite for this level of warfare."

"That brings us back to square one again," said Fingimiento angrily. "Why should we trust your choice?"

"Yes, and who is to say the rest of the territories will be split evenly once the FADF has been annihilated," said Flores.

And so the meeting continued for hours with its petty bickering and singular lack of trust between any of the Syndicate members. And, as usual, there was no firm outcome by the end. It was this inherent distrust and incessant squabbling that was the chink in their armour - their single biggest weakness.

"Perhaps we should call a close to this summit," Glace finally suggested. "We seem to be going round in circles again. Everyone should have time to ponder the possibilities, how each of our skills can work in unison, after all we know the FADF will be no pushover - and planning will be the key to our success."

"Agreed," said Oro. "Why don't we all retire for the evening? We can talk again tomorrow. My sister will show you to your quarters and organise refreshments."

"As long as the food is better than that rabbit food your chef tried to feed me earlier," said Espectro gruffly. "I'm starving!"

Chapter Three
LILY ROSE

Once the others had gone, Oro signalled to his sister that he wished to be left alone. He went to his desk and opened one of the drawers, taking out a small wrapped box tied up with a ribbon. He smiled, putting it in his top pocket and walked over to a large bookcase at the back of the huge office. He pushed on a dusty volume entitled 'Magnificent Marvels and Obscure Oddities' and part of the bookcase slid back to reveal a heavy oak door. He took a key from around his neck and unlocked it, climbing the narrow staircase that led up to an isolated tower. He was somewhat out of breath by the time he reached the top and unlocked another door leading into a room. The room was large and circular, dark like a night without stars due to the fact that there were metal grids on all the windows. A maid stood up and bobbed a hasty curtsy to Oro.

"Mr Cazador, I didn't realize you were coming to visit today. Can I get anything for you?"

"No, leave us. I will call when I want you."

The maid bolted out like a frightened rabbit, shooting a quick glance behind her.

In the centre sat a beautiful, if not rather sad looking girl surrounded by sparrows who also took flight upon his entrance. Her long hair was carefully combed and adorned with fresh flowers. The girl's complexion was creamy, her lips like strawberries and her eyes were almost ocean blue. She turned her head back to look out of the window, watching the birds sail off into the distance.

"Lily, are you not glad to see me? Do you not have a kiss for your beloved father?" he said, his expression softening.

The girl stood up slowly and walked over to where he stood, kissing him chastely on the cheek. "How are you Papa?"

"All the better for seeing my beautiful daughter. Look, I have a present for you, something that will put a smile on that pretty face of yours." He held out the box to her but she did not take it.

She simply walked over to one of the barred windows again and gazed out longingly. "The gardens look so beautiful at this time of day with the evening sun streaming down."

"Aren't you going to open your present Lily? It's really special...look I'll do it for you."

He carefully opened the box taking out a stunning toy bird with feathers of woven gold, and tiny precious gems.

"I commissioned it especially for you...look it has a key here and when you wind it up...listen it sings so sweetly!"

She turned around, a silhouette against the window. "I don't want anymore presents Papa...I want to go outside...I can't bear being stuck in this room any more. It's a prison...and I'm suffocating!"

Oro sat down heavily in a chair and looked at her. "Not this again! Don't be so melodramatic," he growled. "I have told you a million times, it is for your own good, for your own protection – the whole of The Syndicate is here and I couldn't bear it if anything happened to you."

"It won't and besides those people are meant to be your friends."

"I have explained to you before, I have to work with these

people, they are not friends. They would soon as destroy me if it meant they could get their hands on my lands and riches. It is better you stay here."

"I don't want to. Please Papa…I just want to go for a walk in the garden. I'm begging you!"

"No! Don't ask me again!"

"But why?"

He sighed heavily. "I am a powerful man and powerful men have many enemies, enemies that would try anything to get to me…you are the most precious thing in my life…I can't take that risk…I'm just doing what any good father would do…protecting you Lily. Zartarbia is a dangerous place…these are treacherous times my darling child. Please Lily, don't work yourself up so…"

"I'm not a child anymore! I'm almost grown up…I want to see the world."

"You should be content with what you have. You have every luxury imaginable, dresses made from diamonds, shoes made from the softest leather, flying coats of birds and butterflies…"

"And what for, where can I fly to?"

"I give you everything you want. No other man can look after you the way I do…"

"You don't give any other man the opportunity!" she retorted. "One day I will want to marry and have children of my own."

"I won't hear such nonsense…you are far too young to talk of such things! When the appropriate time comes I will find a suitable husband for you – somebody to suit your social standing."

"No! Don't you get it? I want to marry for love not because you have chosen somebody that is powerful or wealthy…I don't care about those things – love is what is important and the freedom to be myself…!!!!"

"Love is a dangerous affliction. Listen to me I am simply protecting you my darling…after your mother passed away…"

"She didn't pass away! She was killed!" Lily said bitterly, shooting a sideways look at her father. She had often wondered if her father had anything to do with her mother's sudden death, but couldn't believe this of him. That would be too evil even for him!

"That is enough! I am your father and I won't have you speaking to me like that!"

Lily suddenly ran at her father, beating her fists on his chest. "I'm not one of you're stupid possessions to be kept behind glass…you can't keep me prisoner forever! I hate you!" she screamed.

Oro grabbed his daughter's hands. "Stop this right now! This behaviour is most unbecoming."

The girl jerked herself away from him, sobbing uncontrollably.

"I'm leaving now Lily. You have upset me greatly. I think you need time to reflect on your erratic behaviour. I shall leave your present on the table."

Oro left the room, locking the door behind him. Lily cried out in frustration and picking up the toy bird, she threw it at the closed door, smashing it. She slid down to the floor, tears staining her porcelain skin.

The maid returned quietly locking herself into the room with Lily. She went over to her mistress, trying to comfort her. "Oh don't cry mi'lady, please don't cry."

"I hate him! I really hate him Lauren!" said Lily wiping her eyes angrily.

"There, there…come now," said the maid handing her a handkerchief. "Dry those pretty eyes."

"I have to get out…I can't bear this any more – being cooped up day after day."

She suddenly grabbed Lauren's sleeve. "There is one way!" she said urgently, her eyes gleaming brightly. "We could switch places, swap clothes! I could run away…get away from this place forever… Oh please Lauren, will you help me? Please I'm going crazy!"

The maid looked horrified at the suggestion. "Mi'lady that's impossible! Your father would kill me…he'd kill my family – you know I can't take that sort of risk! Anyway if you tried to run away he'd have you tracked down within hours."

"I'm begging you, it would be simple…alright…I won't run away, I just want to feel the sun on my face," said Lily urgently, "even just for a few moments."

"I want nothing more than your happiness mi'lady but I can't help you. Please don't ask me again. Truly I hate seeing you like this but you know what your father would do if he found out."

Lily nodded and though disappointed by Lauren's refusal, she understood the maid's terror of her father. Out of the forty six maids who had cared for her in the past seventeen years, forty three had been murdered on Oro's command. Usually their 'crimes' were trivial, like dressing Lily in the wrong gown when her father had dictated she wore another, or for having trimmed Lily's hair without his permission, or even for something as banal as not arranging the folds of the curtains in a certain way. Every morning a list of specific instructions were sent up and if they were not followed exactly, the maid paid with her life. Lily had no choice but to obey her father, for fear of the consequences.

She was very aware of what a brutal and excessive man her father was. Since her mother died he had re-married many times and each of his unfortunate, and extremely wealthy, wives had suffered the same fate…death. Oro hated and mistrusted all women, but he loved money and, once he had persuaded each wife to entrust all their wealth to himself, they were imprisoned in a dungeon in the depths of his castle.

"I feel terrible mi'lady, really I do," Lauren said clasping the girl's hand.

"It's alright. I don't know what I was thinking of. I'm sorry," said Lily smiling sadly. "We are both his prisoners."

Chapter Four
THE PROPOSITION

Oro slowly walked down the staircase and back into his private office, feeling most agitated. A huge fire had been lit and Glace was waiting for him. She immediately noticed his face was as dark as thunder. He sat down and poured himself a large glass of Amenesian

"Brother, what is vexing you? Is it the girl again?"

"My daughter has a name - why do you never use it, woman!" he barked.

"She has upset you I presume…she is of course at that age," said Glace. "Did she not like the gift?"

"She told me she hated me."

"I see," said his sister, her reptilian eyes flickering.

"I am her father! How dare she?!!!"

"Brother, she is no longer a child – she grows more like her mother every day…there will come a day when you will have to relinquish control of her…"

"Shut your foul mouth!" Oro turned abruptly downing his drink in one. "Anyway what the hell do you want?" "Devin Fortuno wishes a private audience with you," she replied. "I told him you were busy but he insisted. He is waiting in the next room."

"What does the damn fool want?"

"He says he has a proposition for you that you will be most interested in."

"I doubt that very much."

"Do you want me to send him away?"

"No show him in."

Glace turned from her brother and opened the adjoining doors. "Mr Fortuno, my brother has agreed to see you. Come this way."

Devin settled himself into an armchair opposite Oro Cazador and poured himself a drink. "Hope you don't mind," he said flippantly, "but the service here leaves a lot to be desired."

"Just get on with what you have to say Mr Fortuno…"

Devin strummed his fingers lazily against the arm of the chair. "I have a proposition for you…"

"Yes, yes, I know that…my sister has just informed me…so let's not beat about the bush…what is it?" snapped Oro impatiently.

"I know of a way that you can control all of Zartarbia."

Oro snorted with laughter, "Oh very droll."

"No seriously…I have something in my possession that would give you power over The Syndicate and the FADF. In due course you will have all their territories – just hear me out," said Devin, stroking his beard.

"Go on," said Oro darkly, his glass eye glinting in the firelight.

"You're aware I own a small land called Sumptitious..."

"It's worthless. Is this all you want to discuss with me?"

"To the uneducated eye, yes I agree, but within this territory is the Hotel Gastronomic and the chef there creates food that has power over whoever eats it. Admittedly it is a temporary power but it will give you enough time to gain control of the other Syndicate members – I mean, let's face it, nobody can work together…that's clear enough from today's meeting. This is your chance to take control."

"Go on," said Oro pouring himself another drink.

"The chef creates such culinary delights that bring out emotions you didn't think you had! This food is like a drug, you have no control over who you are anymore. It is impossible to resist," he drawled, circling the rim of his glass with a finger.

"I have never heard of this hotel."

"It's a well kept secret. Naturally I can provide proof – you only have to say the word and I shall arrange a visit for you."

"So what's in it for you? That is, if what you say is correct."

"Once you have The Syndicate under your power, then the FADF will be just as easy to manipulate. You know I don't like to get my hands dirty. It is up to you, but if you accept my offer I want a 30% share of the remaining Zartarbian territories. I'm sure we can reach an accord as to which ones…"

"We'll see."

"I know what you are thinking - why don't I just use this myself, why involve you?"

"The thought had crossed my mind," said Oro leaning back on his chair.

"You're not a stupid man Oro, quite the opposite. I know we have not always seen eye to eye but I respect you, so I will level with you my friend - I am lazy, it is in my nature and it doesn't suit my lifestyle to take risks."

"Where's the risk if everything you say is true?"

"I suppose what I meant is that I do not have the necessary skills, but you do," he paused, rubbing his hands together. "There is a lady involved… I know that your charm is legendary when it comes to women. She is the proprietor of the hotel and the chef is her son… she would need some persuasion but that shouldn't be difficult for you."

"So you don't own this hotel?"

"I do - because I own Sumptitious and all the people that reside there. I am simply saying that Dorian Glittergold would be much more amenable to your plans if she were to…how shall I put this?...find herself in a position of affection for you? I am married so naturally any romantic involvement is out of the question but you are unattached. Let's face it, what's one more wife to secure your future as King of Zartarbia?"

"And what's to stop me not turning on you after the deal is done?" said Cazador slowly.

"I might be idle my dear friend, but I am not the total fool you think me to be. I have the cure for these delicious maladies."

"What do you mean exactly?" said Oro, his face furrowing into a scowl.

"I would never offer such a powerful weapon to you without safeguarding myself against the possibility that you would betray me. I have the only antidote which counter balances the effects of this food…and there is one other thing."

"What is that?" said Oro warily .

"You have The Box of Reversals I believe?" said Devin nonchalantly.

"What makes you say that?"

"You are a collector of rare and precious things and, I have been reliably informed."

"By whom?"

"You know I won't reveal my sources…let's just put it this way, it should by rights be mine, it was promised me. After Sectica died, it vanished and I knew that if anybody had it, it would be you."

Oro Cazador narrowed his piggy eye, the glass one fixed on the Soothsayer. "You know of course that it is useless without the other elements…"

"Of course, everybody knows that," replied Devin, clasping his hands together.

"So why do you want it?"

"Let's just put it this way, one never knows when one's luck is about to change…it is, after all, an extremely valuable item. If I was to fall on hard times, and believe me when I say my wife spends money like water…I have to have a little something for a rainy day."

"I'm not sure. I need time to think."

"What have you to lose? Look, don't trust my word. Go and see for yourself, because as they say, the proof is in the pudding."

"I said I shall think about it!" snapped Oro.

"I wouldn't think for too long…besides I'm sure the food would be a wonderful remedy for your daughter's current disposition…" drawled Devin, draining the rest of his drink and standing up.

"What are you talking about?"

"I overheard the conversation between you and your charming sister," he replied.

"How dare you! That was private!"

"Please, I am simply saying it could be a solution for more than one of your problems…that's all." He turned to go. "Well, I shall retire to bed and let you think things over. We'll speak more tomorrow. Goodnight Oro and er…thanks for the drink!" With a swirl of his long coat Devin Fortuno vanished, leaving Oro Cazador to sit mulling over his suggestion.

Chapter Five
A PLOT IS HATCHED

It was the following evening before Oro finally had the opportunity to discuss Devin's proposition with his sister. The day had been gruelling, filled with bitter arguments between all The Syndicate members. They were both relieved when the members had finally departed.

"I've organised for us to take dinner in the main study," said Glace. "Do you want me to summon the girl to join us?"

"No, not tonight. I will see Lily later. I want to speak to you in private about something," he said rubbing the back of his neck.

"Well, let's talk over supper," suggested Glace.

They walked through to the study, which was an austere room that was sparsely decorated. One wall was completely covered with television screens, from which Oro could keep an eye on every corner of his empire.

Naturally all the guest rooms had been bugged, as had all the staff quarters, and information on The Syndicate was currently being collated by Betrug Espion.

They sat down as a trail of servants entered with various platters heaving with food. Oro helped himself to a huge portion of creamy pasta, followed by an entire chicken pie with three plates of chips, finished off with a massive bowl of trifle and a plate of Turkish Delight. Glace, in contrast, picked at a small salad.

"So what did Mr Fortuno want?"

"Well that's what I wanted to discuss with you," he said, speaking with his mouth full.

"He says there is a chef in Sumptitious that can create food that can control people's feelings. He claims we could use it to influence The Syndicate's decisions and take control of their territories in due course."

"Why have we not heard of this chef before? If such a person exists we would have known of it."

"Not necessarily…Sumptitious is a small and insignificant country…a very self contained place."

"How do you know this is not some sort of scam? You know what the man is like!"

"He says he will provide proof."

"If this food is so powerful then why doesn't he use its magic himself?"

"He's lazy. He wants somebody else to do all the work and then he can take his share of the spoils."

"I'm not convinced! He is a devious trouble maker and I don't trust him."

"I agree, but I think it would be worth our while to at least check out his claims. The Syndicate is split. If I had the power to take control, just imagine how much I could achieve – the whole of Zartarbia could be mine!" he declared, curling his hand into a fist.

"So what does he want in return?" said Glace, dabbing delicately at her mouth with a napkin.

"30% of territories, but I think I can get him down on that…he wants a quiet life and the assurance I will leave him alone."

"What makes you think you can negotiate with him? Suppose

he has already approached say Espectro or Tempest?"

"He wants The Box of Reversals, that's why he's come to me…"

"How does he know you have The Box of Reversals? Who told him? There must be a leak in our security!"

"No. It was a member of Sectica's staff who took it just before her mansion was destroyed. Betrug found out earlier on today."

"The box is useless without the other elements, nobody even knows where half of them are, and the human child took The Locket of Fire and Water back to her own world…so what does he know that we don't?"

"I'm not sure, but I will find out. Let us first see if his claims are correct. Besides, Lily could do with a trip away and I believe the change will do her good. I shall leave the arrangements to you," he said. "I shall go and tell her the good news now. That should lift her spirits."

Meanwhile elsewhere in Zartarbia…

Devin Fortuno and Opal Luvie were relaxing in their gigantic palace, being entertained by belly dancers and fire-eaters. The large salon was lined with piles of velvet cushions and the room was alight with music and laughter. Various friends of the couple lounged around being fanned with huge fans by numerous servants, whilst other slaves fed them grapes or poured them another drink. The air swirled with incense and the revellers were clearly enjoying the decadent party.

Opal was draped across her husband. "So my love, do you think he will take the bait?"

Devin grinned wolfishly. "It's just a matter of time. Cazador's appetite is whetted and he won't want to pass up on at least checking out The Hotel Gastronomic…and once he is there, the food will convince him and we shall have the Box of Reversals."

"And what of the girl? Can you see when she will return to Zartarbia?"

Devin spun his hand across a crystal ball, watching it light up. Within the glowing centre Isabella's face emerged.

Devin turned to his wife. "It will be soon my darling...very...very soon and when she comes back we shall have The Locket of Fire and Water, as well as the Box of Reversals. Then we can set the rest of the plan in action."

"It will be so much fun playing them off against one another," purred Opal. "I shall enjoy watching them doing all the dirty work, but not as much as I will enjoy being Queen of Zartarbia!"

"We must be patient my love, it will all take time."

She kissed him. "I can wait...especially now that stupid woman, Sectica, is out of the way. You really were so clever knowing that the locket would destroy her. That was a stroke of pure genius!"

"We still have five more to get rid of and it will take a lot of skill and cunning to manipulate them."

"If anybody can do it then it's you my darling...you are so deliciously devious!"

Chapter Six
RETURN TO RAVENTHORPE

It was autumn time before Isabella visited Raventhorpe again, the home of her eccentric Great Aunt Cisely, which she also ran as a small private school for children. Isabella's parents visited Raventhorpe during the school holidays, and Isabella looked forward to it every time. She loved the worn splendour, the warmth of the large sitting room where her great aunt used to tell her stories in front of the fireplace, whilst Isabella toasted marshmallows. She also loved exploring the myriad of passageways leading to so many rooms – some known to her, and some unknown. These were cold, untouched rooms during the holidays although brought to life during the term time by the happy voices of children. Unlike the attic upstairs which remained unvisited, apart from the spiders that spun their webs from beam to box and back again. The attic and its many treasures remained silent and waiting…

It seemed like an age before Isabella and her parents reached Darlington and had finally turned into the gravel driveway that led to the school.

The trees were an explosion of bright colours, their leaves glowing orange and red, the light falling between life and decay.

Berries nestled in bushes, a sharp contrast to the grey sky above. It was half term at the school so they had the place to themselves, providing Isabella plenty of opportunity to explore all the interesting nooks and crannies. Only the staff remained to clean and prepare meals, as Aunty Cis was the worst cook in the world. She had tried to boil an egg once and managed to set fire to the entire kitchen! Luckily a neighbour had called round for a glass of sherry and been able to help her put out the flames. It was just as well her great aunt could afford to have staff, as she was hopelessly undomesticated.

On another occasion she had attempted to iron a blouse but rather than use an ironing board she had decided to do it on the carpet. Naturally the carpet was ruined but, rather than admit her mistake, she simply dragged a chair over to cover the scorch marks.

She could also be dreadfully forgetful - "Now where have I put my glasses?" she'd ask. "They're on your head," Isabella would reply with a giggle.

However, it had to be said that Aunty Cis was very different from most elderly people and Isabella adored her. For example, she liked to slide down banisters when there were no other adults around to raise a disapproving eyebrow. She would argue with the television, telling off newsreaders if she didn't like what they were reporting or if she thought they looked scruffy. "Well really!" she'd say, "If I had a pair of scissors, I'd climb through the screen and give that fellow a decent haircut!"

She was also a big fan of picnics and they would often venture outside Darlington onto the Yorkshire Dales to find a hollow on a wind-blown mountainside. Here they would set up their picnic and sit munching egg mayonnaise sandwiches together.

They were in the sitting room when Aunty Cis sneezed, not just once but seven times in a row, as she always did! Isabella's mother

Isabella Zophie and Aunty Cis having tea at Ravenhorpe.

had been trying to persuade Aunty Cis to drink all sorts of foul tasting medicines.

"You really should let me telephone Doctor Newman. You've had that cold for over a month now," remarked Isabella's mother as she sipped her tea.

Aunty Cis blew her nose noisily and shook her head. "Don't fuss so dear, it's the weather that's all!" She returned to the crossword which she had been busy puzzling over. "Right then six across…the clue is overweight in stature, with part of the word forming the name of an alcoholic beverage. Umm, another word for overweight…six letters…chubby, chunky, flabby…no…an alcoholic beverage…stout! No that's only five letters…oh bother...."

"Portly," interjected Isabella's mother. "Port being the alcoholic beverage."

"Ah yes, of course it is," she said as she filled in the boxes and then neatly folded up the newspaper. "Well that will do for now. Isabella, would you like another biscuit?"

Isabella looked at her mother. "No, she's had quite enough and she won't eat her lunch otherwise. Now, I'm going to see where your father has got to Isabella."

The moment Isabella's mother had left the room, Aunty Cis sneakily slid over another biscuit, grinning defiantly. "What's life for if you can't enjoy it? The trouble with parents is that they forget you're only a child for such a short time… Oh! I tell you what would be fun. We should arrange a midnight feast!" she said excitedly, adding. "How about tonight?"

"That would be great!" exclaimed Isabella, her eyes shining.

Aunty Cis sneezed seven times again. "Oh bother this cold. Look I tell you what, I'll bring the sweets and sneak over to your room so that way, if your parents are still awake, I'll simply say I thought you were having a bad dream…and they'll be none the wiser! Besides, I've a huge cupboard full of chocolates that the school children's parents keep giving me…I'll never get through the whole lot by myself. Deal partner?" she said mischievously, sticking out her hand.

"Deal partner," giggled Isabella, shaking hands on their pact.

"What are you two whispering about?" asked Isabella's mother who had suddenly reappeared in the doorway with her father.

"Oh nothing," said Isabella, trying not to look guilty.

"I was just saying that, as the weather doesn't look as if it's going to cheer up, I might take Isabella shopping in town this afternoon," said Aunty Cis cheerily.

"Well your father and I have a few bits and pieces to do anyway, so I could drop you both at the department store and pick you up later. But is it wise for you to be going out when you're unwell?"

"I'm fine! It's just a silly sniffle that's all!"

"All the same, you need to keep warm."

"Yes, yes I will!" Aunt Cis agreed impatiently. She checked her watch before announcing happily, "Cook is serving lunch in about half an hour, so it's time for a sherry. I'm quite parched now."

"I'll do the honours," said Isabella's father, as he poured out three glasses on the drinks cabinet.

They sat and chatted for a while until Cook sounded the dinner gong. They all crossed the huge hallway that was lined with empty coat pegs, each with a pupil's name and picture above it, and entered into the dining room. This room also acted as an Assembly Hall during term time, so the walls were adorned with various pictures and letters of the alphabet. It was a massive room, almost as big as a small flat, the huge windows were partially covered with net curtains. Isabella inhaled deeply as she caught a whiff of furniture polish. It had obviously been the housekeeper, Mrs Plum's day to clean it. But the smell of furniture polish was quickly replaced by the smell of hot food as Cook wheeled in a squeaky trolley, assisted by Mrs. Plum who smiled warmly at them.

"You've roast beef with Yorkshire puddings, mashed potato, carrots, peas and cauliflower cheese…the gravy's in the jug here and I've done an apple crumble with custard for afters," Cook said sharply as she slammed the dishes down.

Isabella had never seen two more opposite people than Cook and Mrs Plum. The latter was plump and kindly, the sort of person that could always find a good word to say about everybody; she always had a sparkle in her eyes and a ready smile. Cook, in contrast, was scrawny with a mean face and a terrible temper. She also hated children, which confused Isabella as to why she would have chosen to work in a school.

"Very good Cook," said Aunty Cis perching her well-upholstered backside on a chair. "You may go home now if you wish. Thank you both."

"Are you sure there's nothing else needs doing?" asked Mrs Plum.

"No thank you."

"Well I'll see you tomorrow Mrs Jaques," she said to Aunty Cis.

Cook turned abruptly and walked in a precise fashion out of the room whilst Mrs Plum seemed to bustle her way out. Isabella masked a giggle and gave Mrs Plum a little wave as she reversed out of the room, with another goodbye.

The house seemed eerily quiet after the rest of the staff had left, just the sound of the wind rattling the window panes and the gurgle of the old radiators. Isabella often wondered if her great aunt ever got scared at night time when she was all alone by herself (Uncle Billy, her husband, had passed away some years before). Aunty

Cis always said she wasn't and, indeed, when she once caught a thief in the house, she had frightened him off by hitting him with her walking stick. "The cheek of that young hooligan!" she'd say when she was recounting the incident, "Well he won't do that again in a hurry if he knows what's good for him!"

All the same, she locked herself into her bedroom every night after that.

As with a lot of elderly people, many of her friends and family were dead, such is the nature of old age, but she never complained. Not once. Instead she busied herself with lots of activities, not sky diving or wind surfing (although she would have given it a go except for the arthritis in her knees). Instead, her preferred pastimes included card games and playing the piano. She would warble away at the top of her voice singing Beatles songs (which, for the younger readers, was a very famous pop band in the 1960's – ask your parents as they will know who I am talking about!)

Her favourite was 'We all live in a yellow submarine'.

After a delicious lunch, Isabella's father drove them all into the centre of Darlington and dropped them at Binns, which was a large department store.

"Right, well, I will be back in an hour. Does that give you enough time?" he asked.

"Oh yes, plenty. Come on Isabella," said Aunty Cis. "Let's see if we can find a present for you."

"You mustn't spoil her," said Isabella's mother leaning out of the car window. "Remember Isabella, you're not to ask for anything. You have your pocket money if you want to buy something. See you later."

After they had driven away and were out of earshot, Aunty Cis grinned.

"It's a pity I'm rather deaf in my left ear as I didn't quite catch what your mother said. Never mind, I'm sure it wasn't important." She linked her arm through Isabella's. "Let's go and spend some money."

They had great fun together and Aunty Cis bought her a beautiful diary with a lock on it, a fountain pen and some new clothes.

The rest of the day passed fairly uneventfully and soon it was time for bed. Aunty Cis's cold had got worse and, although she didn't say anything, she was clearly under the weather. They decided to postpone the midnight feast; instead, Isabella fell asleep reading.

Chapter Seven
THE DREAM

It was still dark outside when Isabella woke with a jolt, her heart was racing and she felt curiously troubled. She lay quietly for a few moments, pulling the duvet right up to her chin as if this would keep away the nightmare she had just had. Branches scratched at the window and somewhere in the distance she could hear a dog barking. She switched on her bedside lamp, blinking against the sudden change in light. She clambered out onto the floor and padded down the corridor to where her parents were sleeping, pushing open the creaky door.

"Mama, Papa?" she whispered. "Are you awake?"

"What's the matter darling?" asked her mother sleepily.

"I had a bad dream. Can I come into bed with you?"

"Of course you can. Be quiet though so that you don't wake your father," whispered her mother pulling back the covers. "What did you dream about darling?"

Isabella snuggled up to her mother. "It was really scary. There was a man and he wanted to kill me. He had a glass eye, he was staring at me as if he could read my thoughts…and there was a dungeon full of skeletons. And a boy…except he wasn't. He was covered with fur and scars…he looked so sad and scared."

"You've been watching too much television again," murmured her mother. "Now go to sleep or you'll be tired tomorrow."

The following morning brought voracious winds that blew thin draughts under doors. Isabella's parents had got up early to go to church and left her to have breakfast with Aunty Cis. Isabella followed her great aunt into the bathroom that adjoined the master bedroom, which also acted as a small kitchenette complete with a fridge, cooker and grill. The bathroom was typically old fashioned with a ridiculously high ceiling (which made it very chilly in the winter) and faded flowery wallpaper. As Aunty Cis attempted for the third time to make toast without burning it, in-between fits of sneezing, Isabella got out the butter and marmalade and laid the table in the bedroom. Soon they were sitting in the front of the electric fire munching singed toast and watching cartoons together. After a while a pop band came on to the show to sing their latest hit single.

"Goodness me!" exclaimed Aunty Cis. "That girl has forgotten to put her clothes on, she's dancing around in her underwear. She'll catch her death and, look, she's clearly fallen head first into a pot of paint as well! She's got shocking pink hair and it's all spiky. I'd better telephone the BBC so they can let the poor thing know she's forgotten to wash it out!"

"She's got dyed hair and she's wearing the latest fashion, that's all," giggled Isabella knowing full well this was her great aunt's idea of a joke.

"Well I think there would be more than a few raised eyebrows on Parent's Evening if I wore just my bra and girdle, still I suppose the song is quite catchy. Now, in my day when I was a child…" said Aunty Cis dabbing a dribble of melted butter from her chin, "…we didn't have television, let alone these new fangled gadgets like video machines and computers."

"I couldn't imagine not having a television or computer. Everybody has them!"

"People have too much these days if you ask me. Mark my words, life was better in my youth because it was simpler. Our entertainment was a good book or a jolly sing along. Children were allowed to be children - they grow up too quickly now," she said blowing her nose for the umpteenth time that morning. "Oh this wretched cold!"

"Do you want me to get you anything?" asked Isabella.

"No dear, really I'm fine. When you get to my age, even the smallest ailment takes its toll unfortunately. Anyway, where were we?...Ah, yes, childhood, you must make the most of it Isabella."

"But when you're a child, adults boss you around the whole time and your parents always think they're right even if they're not! I can't wait to grow up."

"Oh my dear child, you mustn't wish time away – you have the rest of your life to be an adult and only a short time left to be a child. You must enjoy that time, it will never return. It's one of the reasons I love having a school so much, you see, it's the children that keep me young at heart."

"Tell me the story again about how you came to be a teacher," said Isabella, cupping her hands around a mug of steaming tea.

Aunty Cis would often say she would have liked to have been an actress but had ended up working as a teacher by accident.

"Surely you must be bored hearing that old story?" said her great aunt, peering over the top of her glasses.

"No, I like hearing about you and Granny Mop – please…" Isabella begged, tucking her feet up on the chair.

"Alright then, if it will make you happy," she said refilling her teacup. "Do you want some more toast before I start?"

Isabella shook her head, "No thank you."

"Or cereal? I've some cornflakes in the cupboard if you're still hungry."

"I'm full, really I am. Tell me the story, I really want to hear it again."

"Well if you insist," Aunty Cis sat back and her eyes misted up with memories of the past. "It was many years ago now… my mother died when I was a child and Father had re-married this dreadful woman. We called her Ginge because of her red hair and her penchant for gin. None of us liked her and I don't suppose she much liked us, but Father was besotted with her and he did everything that ghastly woman said. So one day I decided to run away. All I needed was a bit of money – and I knew where Father kept his cheque book. I have always been rather good at forging his signature! Of course he was furious when he found out, but by then it was too late."

"Did he shout at you?"

"No. He was too controlled for that, he simply washed his hands of me. Anyway, I had a friend who owned a hat shop and I quite liked the idea of making hats. It seemed quite an adventure at the time."

"Then she took all your money and made you work like a slave," chipped in Isabella eagerly.

"Who is telling this story?" said Aunty Cis sharply, but the twinkle in her eye belied the tone of her voice. Isabella grinned and pretended to zip up her mouth.

"Yes, well I was young and naïve. She made me work day and night. I was too stubborn to go back to Father with my tail between my legs, but I had nowhere else to go. Anyway, every day I had to walk past Raventhorpe on my way to work and I would often see Granny Mop in the garden, pruning the roses. She was quite a famous writer in those days, that's how she could afford to live in such a huge house. She'd wave and I'd wave back. By this stage I had carbuncles on my eyes from all the late nights working in poor light…I looked quite a sight! Then one day we started chatting. Well! I can tell you, she was horrified when I told her about the hat shop and insisted then and there that I go and live with her."

"Just like that?" asked Isabella.

"Just like that. So we sat down over a nice cup of tea and she told me she thought I would make a good teacher, and that she had been thinking of turning Raventhorpe into a school, she said after all it could be easily converted into classrooms. I had never taught before in my life…I just sort of learned on the job – as people often did back then - and the rest is history."

Outside the sound of a car could be heard on the gravel driveway.

"Your parents are back if I am not mistaken," said Aunty Cis. "I had better wash these plates up."

"I'll do it…I don't mind," said Isabella clearing them away.

"You're a good girl," smiled her great aunt who then promptly started sneezing again. "Oh dear this cold seems to be getting worse."

A few days later, Aunty Cis's health had not improved, in fact it had got progressively worse. The cold had spread to her chest and, though Isabella's father had to return down South for work, her mother had stayed to nurse her aunt. Doctor Newman had paid several house calls and insisted that she be confined to bed, as she was in danger of developing full blown pneumonia.

Aunty Cis was sleeping when Isabella entered the master bedroom and her mother was talking in lowered tones on the phone. "No, she's a little better but I expect to be here for a least another three or four days…yes…well it's just one of those things…"

"Mama?"

"Sorry hang on one moment…What is it?" her mother said sharply, covering the mouth piece with her hand. "Can't you see I'm busy?"

"I'm bored. Can I go outside to play?"

"Don't be so silly, it's raining. The last thing I need is for you to get ill as well – now off you go and amuse yourself! Yes, sorry…no it's just my daughter…oh you know what children are like…yes, isn't it just…"

"What shall I do?" asked Isabella miserably, feeling rather neglected.

"Isabella, you can see I'm talking to somebody!"

"It's not fair…you never have time for me!" she said angrily, feeling hurt.

"I'm not in the mood for sulkiness…now go off and do some drawing or something – I'm trying to make sure that the neighbours are aware of her illness – so stop bothering me!" said her mother irritably, her hand covering the mouthpiece again.

"I'm not. You're so horrible to me!" retorted Isabella.

"You're behaving like a stroppy teenager! I don't know what's got into you!…no I'm still here…yes well I'll call before I have to go home and if you could just pop in and check she's taking her medicine…"

"Well…well I wish you weren't my mother!!! Maybe another mother might have more time to spend with me!" shouted Isabella and with that she stormed out of the room.

Chapter Eight
JANGLE

Isabella went to her bedroom fighting back tears. She half expected her mother to follow, to tell her off for her outburst, but she did not. She decided she would punish her mother - maybe she would hide so that she would worry, perhaps regret the way she had treated her. It was with this thought that Isabella entered the attic once again.

Upon reaching the top of the stairs she quickly recognised the same chaotic clutter of interesting objects that were there before, as she made her way along the carpeted pathway towards the dressing up room. She hesitated before drawing back the curtain, pausing for a moment to think that maybe she should go back down to her mother and try to make up - but then again why should she? She was not the one at fault! Defiantly she entered the small room, looking for something in particular – The Locket of Fire and Water.

Isabella somehow felt that she was home the moment she stepped into the dressing room, with its walls lined with costumes – monsters and fairies; soldiers and ballerinas; queens and waiters; wings and swords. She sat herself down by the large wooden trunk that had previously contained the locket, wondering if her great aunt had put it back inside. She had said that Isabella could wear it again. She absent-mindedly picked up an old mirror, observing her dusty reflection. Isabella opened the lid of the wooden chest to see it was packed with neatly folded outfits. She pulled them out one by one until the inside was empty. She was just thinking to herself, 'well the locket must be elsewhere', when she noticed a small drawer at the base of the trunk that was ajar. She lifted back the catch, tingling with anticipation and sure enough there was the locket. Its beauty had not diminished nor, she suspected, had its power. She picked it up marvelling at the glitter of its stunning jewels.

She wondered whether it would work a second time, whether Zartarbia was really a place she had visited – in the cold light of day it just seemed like a dumb fairy story. She fastened the locket around her neck and pulled the curtain back again fully expecting for the bathroom on the other side to have vanished, as it had before, but everything was exactly the same.

'I don't understand,' she thought. 'I didn't do anything differently.'

She flopped down onto the floor, feeling even more dejected than before.

"Pppsssttt!"

"Who's there?" Isabella said spinning around but there was nothing.

After a few moments of silence she convinced herself she had just imagined it. 'Well I had better be getting back downstairs,' she thought.

"Ppppssssttttt!!!! I'm over here!" said a high chirpy voice.

Isabella practically jumped out of her skin. "Who are you and where are you?…I'm not scared you know!"

"Well of course you're not scared! There's nothing to be scared of. Look I'm inside the chest…Chop! Chop! We've got work to do!"

Isabella Zophie discovers Jangle in the attic.

Isabella spun round back towards the trunk and looked inside. "I can't see you."

"I'm in the corner. Look I'm here," said the voice.

She peered more carefully and sure enough there was an old iron key with an ornate handle lying in the dust. She picked it up. "Well hello there."

The key suddenly seemed to grow arms and a face melted out of the metal.

"Charmed to make your acquaintance. I'm Jangle," said the key shaking her finger. "So you're the chosen one... you're smaller than I expected."

"I'm Isabella. Are you from Zartarbia?"

"In a manner of speaking. I'm here to help you, so pick me up and let's get going!"

"But I put the locket on and nothing happened."

"You are not necessarily going to enter Zartarbia the same way every time. It depends on the configuration of the gateways."

"The what?"

"Configuration...it means arrangement of the doorways into Zartarbia. It's complicated."

"Are we going back to the circus?"

"The circus?"

"Yes, Le Cirque de Magique, it's where I was the last time I entered Zartarbia."

"I've no idea. I shouldn't have thought so as the Zartarbian lands constantly move and change. One never knows where one will turn up. Now then we really must get going."

Isabella got up and pulled back the curtain again, but this time there was a long dark tunnel that stretched out in front of her and the floor was studded with a strip of tiny lights that seemed to go on forever. The ceiling was dripping with stalactites.

"I can barely see anything," said Isabella dubiously.

"You'll be fine… just follow the lights."

Isabella walked forward, not liking the cold, damp atmosphere of the cave. Her echoing footsteps were the only sound that could be heard. After a while she could faintly make out what appeared to be a door in the distance, it's frame leaking warm light and giving it shape.

"We're almost there," said Jangle as they approached the door.

Isabella tried the handle but it wouldn't open.

"It's locked," she said.

"That's where I come in, now hold me close to the lock and let me have a look."

Jangle examined it for a while, changing the teeth of the key to fit inside the lock. "There we go! That should have done it – try again."

Sure enough Isabella turned the handle and the door opened onto what can only be described as a scene of utter chaos. She found herself in some sort of cloakroom. Through a crack in the curtains she could see numerous waiters running backwards and forwards carrying huge trays laden with food and somebody was shouting orders. She pushed her way through the coats.

"So what now?" she asked Jangle.

"You're guess is as good as mine," shrugged the key. "I suppose we go in."

Isabella was just about to step through the curtains into what seemed to be a hotel reception area when a hand grabbed her, yanking her backwards…

Chapter Nine
THE RAT CHILD

"What do you think you're doing!"

Dorian Glittergold's robust figure suddenly appeared in the darkened doorway.

She hurriedly locked the heavy kitchen door behind her and waddled over to where a trembling figure stood by the open door of a huge fridge. The creature quickly hid behind the door in the shadows.

"I'm sorry stepmother," a frightened voice stammered, cowering further away from her. "Don't you ever call me that! How many times do I have to tell you!" she shouted. "Are you completely stupid! You call me Ma'am if you address me, do you understand?"

"Yes Ma'am, I'm sorry, I forgot Ma'am," he said, his eyes wide with fear.

"Don't look at me you revolting freak! You vile little monster! Stealing again I see!" she raged, yanking the frail form of her stepson out into the moonlight. She lowered her spiteful, flabby face towards the child and slapped him hard. He fell back onto the cold tiled floor.

"You disgust me, look at yourself nobody could love anything as grotesque as you!" She slammed the metal fridge door closed and dragged him up, forcing him to look at himself in the shiny surface. The reflection that stared back was indeed an ugly one, part child, part monster with nervous opaque eyes. A creature covered in patches of coarse hair, such as the type you would expect to see on an animal. Where the skin could be seen it was scarred and scratched from the numerous beatings his vile stepmother inflicted on him. His ragged body was as pale as a bone.

His ears were large and torn, his mouth deformed beyond recognition.

The child tried to raise his hands to cover his face but Dorian prised them away, shoving his face against the mirrored door.

"I think you need reminding of the despicable sight that greets me everyday. See what I have to put up with! You're lucky I have allowed you to stay here, after all nobody else would have you. And how do you repay me?"

She raised herself up, drawing breath for the continued onslaught. "You steal from me! You steal food meant for my precious Tootles!"

(Tootles was Madame Glittergold's pet pig and was, aside from her son Malveo, the apple of her eye. This was the most pampered pig you would ever encounter. He was treated like a king and had his own room, sleeping on satin sheets and eating from gold platters. Tootles was allowed to roam wherever he pleased and far from being dirty, as most pigs are, he was given a warm soapy bath everyday before Dorian Glittergold tied a blue rosette around his hairy neck.)

"Poor Tootles, I dread to think what would have happened if I had arrived a few moments later! You're beneath contempt!" she bellowed, spitting the last few words out.

"I'm sorry Ma'am, please forgive me, it's just that I was so hungry. I haven't eaten anything for three days now….I was only going to have some of the leftovers…"

Before he could say anything else, she gave him a backhander, her heavy ring cutting his cheek.

"Don't answer me back. I tell you when you can eat or not."

He fell down shaking, trying to stem the silent tears that slowly slid through his fur.

"I should turn you out onto the streets to fend for yourself, that's what I should do. I should make you live in the gutter where you belong. Yes, see how you would like that!"

"Oh please no, I'm sorry. I promise not to do it again. I promise not to be bad. Please forgive me!" the boy stuttered rubbing his latest injury, his eyes firmly fixed on his feet.

Dorian Glittergold turned her back to him, patting her hair back into place.

"As punishment you will have nothing to eat for an extra day, no two days. Do you understand?"

She turned, watching his emaciated frame shaking on the floor. He nodded quickly.

"Now get up!" she commanded, slowly picking up a biscuit from a nearby jar, placing it into her rubbery mouth and biting into it noisily, "and you'd better clear up this mess before you go to sleep."

The child looked at his stepmother not understanding, as the kitchen was immaculate, but knowing better than to say anything. She walked purposefully over to the fridge, opening it again and picking out a number of plates of food.

Dorian Glittergold smiled nastily, dipping a finger into a crème brûlé and sucking on it. "Hungry are you?"

He lowered his eyes again, trying not to think how sweet and creamy it would taste within his own mouth. He could feel his mouth salivating at the sight of the delicious delicacies she was holding. His stomach grumbled fiercely, making a loud hollow sound.

"Well I suppose I might have been a touch harsh on you…and you have apologised for trying to steal Tootles' food…perhaps you

Rat Boy

would like some?" she said in a soothing voice. He raised his head, nodding quickly. She held the plate of dessert towards him. "Well come on then! What are you waiting for?"

He was just about to reach out for it when she smashed it on the floor, the sticky mess going everywhere. Again and again she smashed plate after plate of food, shards of glass and crockery splintering across the floor. He scuttled into a far corner.

When the fridges were empty and all the food had been ruined, she finally seemed satisfied.

"Clear this up - and you would do well not to anger me again."

Dorian turned to leave, deliberately walking right through the spoilt food.

"Enjoy your supper," she said sarcastically as she locked him into the kitchen again. She left him in the moonlight, like a ghost with skin.

(As we all know, evil people that deliberately hurt children should be put in jail, which is what should have happened to Dorian Glittergold, but she kept him under lock and key so that nobody guessed her evil secret! Every day, he waited for his chance to escape, to tell someone of his plight, to get help from someone, somewhere. But that day never seemed to come for Isaac, so he was forced to suffer in silence.)

He waited a few moments to hear if she would return, always wary of her cruel games and then, unable to contain himself anymore, picked up a handful of squashed fish and ice cream, devouring it hungrily. He hated himself for doing it but he was so hungry that he would have eaten anything. As he ate, he cut his fingers on the debris of bowls and plates and continued eating until he could no longer stomach the foul tasting mess.

He looked around, feeling exhausted, too tired even to feel sorry for himself.

Suddenly the cutlery began to move, first a spoon and then a whisk. Faces and features appearing through the metal, then arms and legs. One by one they jumped down and hurried over to the boy.

"Oh me poor darlin' child," said a rather plain looking rolling pin, putting a wooden arm around his shoulder. "It's a disgrace that ole cow's behaviour! Let me have a look at that cut. Oi! Master Porcelain, get some warm water and that dishcloth friend of yours."

"Right away Mrs Roly," replied a small round bowl cheerfully, hopping over towards the sink.

"Isaac! Oh me poor luv…we're 'ere dear!" a spatula joined in. "Now don't you worry about all this, we'll 'ave it cleared up in a jiffy. Come on Mr Bristles, Mrs Pan, Moppy and Mr Soapy, we've got work to do."

A broom, dustpan, mop and bucket promptly sprung into action sweeping and washing.

"Thank you, you're so kind to me. I don't deserve it."

"Now stop that preposterous nonsense lad. You mustn't believe those wicked things that old witch says," said an old looking kettle, blowing out angry steam. "She should be locked up for the way she treats you. It ain't right, no child should be treated like that…it's down right evil!"

"I don't know why she hates me so much. I try to be good but nothing I do is ever good enough."

"I know luv, I know. It breaks me heart seein' the way she is towards you."

"What if she throws me out?"

"Oh she won't do that luv, yer too bloomin' valuable to 'er. Her precious 'otel is only successful because of yer cookin' – she knows it and we know it. Yer 'er secret chef. If you go, so does 'er business, straight down the pan!"

A large cooking pot slid over. "Something needs to be done

though, we can't let this continue," he boomed. "It's gone on long enough. She'll end up starving the poor lad to death! That wretched pig gets everything he wants, whilst poor Isaac gets nothing. I can tell you what should be done with that pig, we should make a tasty stew out of him."

"It's not Tootles' fault, he's not to blame," said Isaac sadly. "I just wish my own parents were still alive."

"I know dear, but yer've got us an' we luv yer very much!" said Mrs Roly.

"I think we should escape!" piped up a frying pan.

"We've nowhere else to go, you all know that," replied Isaac.

"I know luv, I know. I wish I could make fings better for yer, we all do," said the rolling pin stroking his fur gently.

The rest of the kitchen utensils clattered their agreement.

"Thanks, I know…it's not the same though."

He turned away, huddling into a cold corner where his bed consisted of a mouldy mattress and a scattering of torn tea towels that acted as a cover.

The magic cutlery sighed and returned to their shelves and cupboards, becoming inanimate objects once again.

Isaac drifted into an uncomfortable sleep that did not last for long, for after a while he became aware of a quiet scrabbling noise, the scratching of claws on the tiled floor.

"Who's there?" he murmured sleepily, raising his head.

The noise increased as about twenty rats scuttled across the floor, surrounding the child.

"Eh, Furry Features, is just us," said one of the rats cheerily.

"We come to see you amigo, we bring regalo, a nice present and we hungry, so what you got uh?"

Now these were not ordinary rats, each was dressed in colourful clothes carefully sewn from discarded socks, sweet wrappers, tiny scraps of leather (or indeed anything these resourceful creatures could get their hands on). They lived in a huge palace deep in the sewers of Sumptitious, where the pickings were often quite plentiful.

(Sumptitious was a land of extremes and excess, where the primary occupation of the wealthy was pleasure seeking but, to support such a lifestyle, there had to be servants at their beck and call. The servants were deliberately kept in poverty by their masters and mistresses. Both sides despised each other but equally they were completely dependent on each other. The rats saw both sides, favouring the down-trodden to the ridiculously pampered. There was no greater extreme than the hideous Madame Glittergold and her poor stepson Isaac. He had always been kind, saving leftover food for them even though he was often hungry himself - a quality afforded them by very few others. In return they would bring him old books and discarded comics to keep him amused in those long lonely hours when he wasn't working. They knew how much he treasured these items as nobody else ever brought him presents.)

"Keep the noise down!" snapped the whisk. "Some of us are trying to sleep, we've got work tomorrow."

"Eh, no worry, chill out…eh rat boy, wake up, you got company! We come to see you eh!" he stood up on his hind legs and took off a large feathered hat, resting a paw against Isaac's arm.

"Don't call him that!" shouted a carving knife, swinging round to face the group.

"He doesn't like it! You call him that again and I'll cut your tail off!"

"Eh Glinty, no offence…is a compliment actually. He like us."

"He's nothing like you," replied the knife sharply. "Anyway you'll get him into more trouble if SHE knows you've been here."

"It's alright Glinty, I don't mind – they don't mean any harm. Capitán Miguel, how are you?" said Isaac.

"Can't complain amigo, but you look a bit peaky. Eh! Carlos, he look offcolour eh, what you think?"

"Si, si. You no look so good!" said Carlos peering into the child's eyes as Isaac propped himself up on his elbows, rubbing the sleep from his eyes.

"Eh, sorry to disturb you but it's like da only time we can see you when we know it safe. I mean after da last time…"

"I know you almost got caught. She's said if she sees you in here again she's going to get a cat…we're going to have to be more careful."

"Hombre, we no scared of her, she just fat lumpy!" said Capitán Miguel defiantly.

"Where's King Pizarro?"

"His royal highness is at der palace but 'e send you dis," said the rat sliding a small book towards the child.

"Thank you. Listen, I'm really sorry but I don't have any food for you as she threw it all on the floor and it's all been ruined…perhaps tomorrow…"

"Actually," said Mr Bristles, the broom. "There's some stuff in that dustbin liner if you don't mind boiled cabbage mixed with leftover chocolate cake."

"Eh, my favourite!" said Capitán Miguel as he scampered over, poking his nose inside.

"Don't make a mess though," said Mrs Pan sternly. "You'll get us all into trouble and we've had quite enough of that for one day."

"Dat true amigo? She give you 'ard time again?" asked Carlos cocking his head.

The boy shuffled into a sitting position rubbing his bruised cheek. "No more than usual."

"She no nice dat lady, we no like!" said another rat called Alfonso.

"No, no she muy mala," the others nodded, all agreeing how bad Dorian was.

"I wish der was something we could do," said Capitán Miguel, stroking his furry beard, "to make it mejor. Better, si!"

"Hey thanks but there isn't. There's nothing anybody can do," said Isaac wearily.

"Listen amigo, dis might cheer you up…we have somet'ing else es para ti, for you my friend," said Capitán Miguel, "as token of our gratitude."

"You don't have to do that!"

"Si, si, we want to!" said Miguel clapping his paws together and twenty more rats appeared carrying with them a hot water bottle. "Eh Steamy! Boil up some water so our young friend here can sleep warmly tonight," he said tapping on the kettle.

"It's great…thank you. Where did you get it from?"

"You ask no question and I tell no lie."

"So yer nicked it then?!!" muttered the rolling pin.

"No Señora Roly, we liberated it for higher purpose, after all we can't have our chico dying of cold. We care about him too, comprende!"

"Yer jist care about yer bellies, yer nothin' more than a bunch of crooks!"

The Capitán stood on his back legs, drawing himself up and puffing out his chest.

"I overlook your rudeness dis once Señora, but you remember you are just chunk of wood, whilst I am da great Capitán Miguel, personal attaché to his majesty King Pizarro Cristibo Eduardo…er, what all 'is names…well no matter, I will overlook der matter dis once - but if happens again, I shall loosen my furious temper on you."

"Yeah and dat es no bueno. Capitán Miguel 'as da verra short fuse and he no like disrespect!" said Carlos wagging his paw at Mrs Roly.

"Whatever, yer don't scare me. Now best yer git out of 'ere, the boy's got a busy day tomorrow, ser clear off!" said Mrs Roly crossly as she turned over.

By now all the magic cutlery was awake and as Steamy poured the scorching hot water into the bottle, each side exchanged winks and smiles as the frail form of the rat boy finally succumbed to the warmest and happiest sleep he had enjoyed in a very long time. Somewhere in the back of his mind he could feel the embrace of his mother, like a half remembered dream.

Chapter Ten
HOTEL GASTRONOMIC

Isabella spun round in a panic, dropping Jangle on the floor….only to find the hand that was gripping her shoulder belonged to her old friend, Lujzka.

"Sshh!" whispered Lujzka, putting her finger to her lips and pulling Isabella through the coats. "Sorry, I didn't mean to scare you."

"You gave me such a fright!" said Isabella, as she picked up the key.

"Ouch!" yelped Jangle. "Be careful! I might be made of metal but I still bruise easily…"

"Sorry," she said dusting the key down. "What are you doing here?"

"I'm on a mission for the FADF, and it's the reason you've been summoned back as well – we need your help. It's good to see you again," said the older girl as she hugged Isabella. "I missed you."

"It's great to see you as well. I wasn't sure I was going to be able to get back in."

"I wasn't sure you were coming, or whether you had received the dream I sent you," said Lujzka.

"The man with the glass eye and the dungeon of skeletons?"

"Yes, Oro Cazador."

"How did you know I would enter here rather than the circus again?" asked Isabella.

"Intuition. Something of you seems to have rubbed off on me after you left to go back to your own world. I see your dreams."

"What all of them?" said Isabella looking surprised.

"Pretty much. Even that one about the jellyfish – that was weird…" said Lujzka grimacing.

"Freaky!" added the key. "So what's the plan?"

"Who is this thing?" she asked Isabella.

"He helped me get in here. His name's Jangle."

"I see. Well he's going to have to stay out of sight for the time being as we don't want to draw attention to ourselves."

"So where are we?"

"In the cloakroom of The Hotel Gastronomic…Now listen carefully Isabella, it has come to our attention that The Syndicate are up to their old tricks, and in particular Oro Cazador."

"Which one is he?"

"He is derived from the sin of Gluttony and is regarded by the FADF as a particularly dangerous Syndicate member. He surrounds himself with the highest levels of security, in fact he rarely leaves his own territories making it next to impossible to place any FADF agents near to him."

"We believe he is arriving here within the next few days and our mission is to discover what he is up to. We know he is meeting Devin Fortuno here, so we all need to be very careful, but you in particular – he knows your face."

"What if he recognises me?"

"Look don't worry, I won't let anything happen to you. You'll be out of sight most of the time. Trust me, alright?" Isabella nodded.

Malveo
~ the revolting son
of Madame Glittergold

"Now we are working undercover so we need to blend in," Lujzka said thrusting some clothes at her. "Put these on as quickly as you can. Our cover is that we are maids from a nearby recruitment agency – it's all been arranged and we already have an agent in position. I'll fill you in with the rest of the details once we have had a chance to meet with her."

Isabella changed into her uniform, whilst Lujzka kept watch through the crack in the curtains. "Are you ready?"

"I guess so." said Isabella shrugging as she tucked Jangle into her apron pocket They quickly stepped through the curtains and into a vast reception area. The smell of the food infiltrated every corner of the hotel, making Isabella's mouth water. Numerous waiters were rushing around and a harassed-looking receptionist was busy answering the phone. Isabella looked around, trying to take in the grand establishment that was – The Hotel Gastronomic.

It was famous locally for its incredible food. Everybody in Sumptitious knew of its reputation and there were always queues of people every night. One had to book months in advance such was its popularity.

It was not just the exquisite flavour of the dishes, nor the unusual combinations of ingredients, nor indeed the intricate attention to detail when it came to presentation – no, although all of these were true, it was something quite different. To taste a mouthful of this food was to feel another emotion altogether, sometimes you would feel such extreme happiness that you would have to grab the nearest stranger and dance around the room, other times you would feel as if you loved everybody in the world. The menus were intoxicating, controlling your body, pulling out all consuming emotions you did not think you possessed, making you forget who you were. Nobody had the power to resist, no matter how bad tempered you might feel beforehand.

Now the other interesting aspect of the hotel was that as guests moved from one room to the other, their clothes changed colour to match the space they were standing in. Even their hair altered colour. It was a most remarkable sight to behold!

For example, the salon was painted a bright red and ladies would stand sipping cherry cocktails, large rubies on their fingers, their crimson evening gowns trailing behind them as they moved around greeting friends. When they walked through to the restaurant, the rubies became sapphires, their elegant dresses transforming into hues of navy, marine and cobalt to compliment the plush blue wallpaper. The library area was decorated in shades of green and the gentlemen that sat smoking after dinner cigars sported smart suits of emerald, moss and lime.

Instruments would play by themselves – flutes and harps circling around a grand piano (which had been fixed to the floor after a rather unfortunate incident when this huge instrument had accidentally knocked over the local Major causing his false teeth to fly out of his mouth and into a nearby bowl of pea soup).

Chairs would automatically pull themselves out for each new guest to sit upon and napkins would unfold with a flourish, settling onto the diner's lap. An enormous staircase led to the upstairs where the guest rooms were situated. Each room was individually furnished to the highest standards and most of the furniture was edible. Beds were made from toffee and nougat; mattresses were made from the softest of soufflés and chairs were carved from fruit cake and iced sponges.

You could even lick the wallpaper – sometimes it tasted of strawberries and cream, other times of lemon sorbet and the flavour never faded (as it does with chewing gum). Now you might be thinking how unhygienic this was, but everything was changed on a daily basis and that was why so many staff were employed. It was also the reason that Lujzka was so certain they could infiltrate the hotel without being detected, and she was right…

"Well don't just stand there gawping! There's work to be done!" bellowed a tall, wiry man striding over to them. His face was narrow and bony. He stared at them with one blue eye and one brown eye, giving him a mis-matched appearance. Everything else about him however, was totally symmetrical from his pin-striped suit to his bowler hat. On his lapel was pinned a badge that said – Spike Pennypinch, Hotel Manager.

Lujzka saw this straight away and said, "Mr Pennypinch, we are from the recruitment agency. We are due to start this evening."

"Not more new staff!" he said rolling his strange eyes. "Does nobody tell me anything around here?!!! Well dinner has already been served some time ago so there's no point you starting now."

"We were told you were expecting us," she replied.

"Well clearly I'm not! Are either of you trained in silver service?" he snapped irritably.

"I'm afraid not…as were hired as maids, not waitresses. We learn fast though."

"I don't have time to babysit new staff. I need people that can get on with things!"

"Mr Pennypinch?" called the receptionist. "Phone call on line two!"

"Can't you see I'm busy, you stupid woman! Tell them to call back!" he shouted.

"They said you were short-staffed," continued Lujzka, "but clearly this is not a convenient time for you. Would you prefer us to come back tomorrow?"

"No…Go to the staff quarters and wait for me there!" he barked and with that, he turned and brusquely walked away.

Lujzka winked at Isabella. "We're in. Follow me." She uncurled her hand which suddenly came to light with a holographic map of the hotel layout. They walked through what seemed to be a labyrinth of corridors, going up and down onto different levels until they finally reached the staff quarters. Lujzka knocked at the heavy wooden door above which hung a fizzing neon sign stating 'STAFF ONLY'.

There was a moment's silence.

"It's very quiet," ventured Isabella. "Maybe everybody's working?"

"Not everybody," she knocked again. "Hello?"

"Who's there?" called a voice.

"Lujzka and Isabella…Mr Pennypinch sent us."

The door creaked open a fraction and the face of a teenage girl peered out. "Quick get in here…I thought you weren't coming. I've been waiting for ages – don't worry there's nobody here except me."

They slipped through the entrance.

"Agent Chloe," said Lujzka, "allow me to introduce you to our secret weapon – Isabella Zophie."

In the meantime…

After a hectic day doing nothing but socialising with the guests and tormenting her stepson, Madame Glittergold was preparing herself for bed. She sat at her dressing table in a pink frilly negligee and matching fluffy slippers. The wig she had worn for the evening had been taken off and been placed alongside the many others. There were wigs in the shape of galleons, some that had been fashioned into fruit and all had been made from the hair of people who were so poor it was one of the last things they had to sell. Not that Dorian Glittergold cared, for she was a selfish woman who was used to getting exactly what she wanted.

Her pet pig, Tootles, was curled up in his comfortable basket, snuffling and snorting from time to time. Downstairs the last of the dinner guests were leaving and the music had faded out.

She had just put a hair net over her receding tresses and was busy applying a thick layer of cold cream to her face when the phone rang in her private quarters.

"Do you know what time it is?" she screeched down the receiver, thinking it was the receptionist or Spike Pennypinch.

"It's Devin Fortuno calling. Apologies for the late hour, my dear Madame Glittergold, I hope I am not disturbing you."

"Oh Mr Fortuno!" she said putting on a posh accent. "What a pleasure to hear from you! How are you and your delightful wife? We haven't had the privilege of your company at Hotel Gastronomic for quite a while."

"It is for that very reason I am calling. I shall be arriving the day after tomorrow and I have invited an extremely important guest to sample some of your culinary delights."

"Oh, how thrilling…who is it?"

"It is essential that you keep this information to yourself as the person in question is extremely security conscious and would not appreciate his privacy being intruded…you will have to clear the hotel of all other guests, other than family of course, and cancel any dinner reservations you have for the next few days."

"Of course, as you know Mr Fortuno, discretion is my middle name!" trilled Dorian (which couldn't be further from the truth, as she was a most terrible gossip).

"This important guest, Mr Cazador, will also expect the highest standards," instructed Devin, who then lowered his voice to convey his next tempting piece of information. "In fact he is visiting Sumptitious because he is interested in acquiring it, and he has heard a lot about your hotel…"

"Mr Oro Cazador?" she interrupted excitedly. "*The Mr Oro Cazador* who owns Glutonious and Segregaria, one of the wealthiest men in Zartarbia?"

"Yes," he replied, glad she had taken the bait. "You understand everything has to be perfect. I want you to organise the most fabulous feast in his honour. I will confirm exact numbers later as I don't know how many will be travelling in his entourage."

"My goodness what an honour! I can hardly believe it! Well naturally I shall put him in the presidential suite…oh how exciting, I shall have to get a new outfit…"

"I am sure he would appreciate that," Devin paused. "As it happens…"

"Yes?" she said breathlessly, urging him on.

"Maybe I shouldn't say anything but, then again, you and he have a lot in common so I will tell you…it has taken him a great deal of time to get over his last wife's death, but I believe he is looking to share his life and his wealth with someone…and I am sure a lady of your charm and beauty would be of great comfort to him…"

"Oh, do you really think so? Do you honestly think a gentleman of his standing would be interested in me?"

"I'm sure you could bring him around….my dear lady, just remember the way to a man's heart is through his stomach – need I say more…"

"No, you need not…I shall look forward to seeing you the day after tomorrow Mr Fortuno."

"Goodbye, and make sure you get plenty of beauty sleep my dear lady!" he said, hanging up the receiver. "She's sure as hell going to need it!" He sneered turning to his wife. Opal laughed, having overheard the conversation. "Like a lamb to the slaughter. You're so good at appealing to people's vanity, my dearest husband."

"It's just a case of knowing what buttons to press," he said kissing her.

Chapter Eleven
AGENT CHLOE

Chloe closed the door behind them. "Come with me as it's not safe to talk here."

She led them through the staff room which, whilst spacious, was not particularly welcoming. It was furnished with long tables and hard wooden benches, with a small fire burning in a brick fireplace at the far end of the room.

"This is where we eat," she explained as she opened another door onto yet another corridor.

"This place is like a maze. I'm never going to remember my way round," said Isabella.

"We're almost there," said Chloe, as she gestured for them to follow her into a small bedroom that looked more like a prison cell with four bunk beds, a single table, stool and stone sink.

She locked the door behind her and removed some sort of scanning device with which she checked the room. "OK, we're all clear. Can't be too careful especially where Cazador's spies are concerned…his usual practice is to send several Transcenders in advance to bug any place he is about to visit."

She pulled a pack out from under her pillow. "You must be

hungry…it's not much but it will keep you going until breakfast."
Chloe held out some rolls, cheese and a flask of water.

"What's a Transcender?" asked Isabella taking a big bite from
the bread.

"A shape changer. They can adopt the physical appearance, voice
pattern and mannerisms of any person," said Lujzka, hitching up her
skirt and unstrapping a wallet that she had concealed underneath a
thick stocking. "They are almost impossible to detect so we should
use a code word to be sure… 263AD89. Here. I've written it down
for you."

She handed the others two tiny pieces of paper. "Now then,
down to business. I have with me several holographic telegrams,"
she handed one to each of them.

"These are only to be used in emergencies as we know Cazador
has developed a sophisticated tracking device which can pinpoint
the sender within the hour. So if you have to use them make sure
you have a clear and fast escape route because you won't have
long. The only place they can be used safely is underground.
Agent Chloe could you update us?"

Chloe sat down on one of the bunk beds. "Well as you know
the proprietor of The Hotel Gastronomic is Dorian Glittergold.
She is a vain, selfish individual as is her only son Malveo. To be
honest neither have much that commends them. Malveo is the
chef here but they are definitely hiding something. Nobody is
allowed to enter the kitchen areas for example, which is odd. I
have heard strange noises coming from inside, even late at night.
The door is kept locked at all times and from what I gather there
is quite a complex alarm system to get through before we even
reach the kitchen."

"Why the excessive security?"

"Exactly. I think whatever the secret Glittergold is concealing could well be connected to Cazador's visit. Sumptitious itself is of little value to him and Devin Fortuno is hardly the most obvious choice of either dinner companion or ally within The Syndicate. They hate each other – so why the meeting and why here?"

"We should not underestimate Fortuno. He plays his cards close to his chest. Detective Valise is still convinced that he had a part in Sectica's death but we have no proof," said Lujzka.

"I'm not so sure I agree. He's no criminal mastermind - but what is certain is that Fortuno must have something that Cazador wants."

"Or he has foreseen Isabella's return and, with her, The Locket of Fire and Water?"

"I doubt it. He would want the locket for himself. Why would he want Cazador to know about it? Besides nobody knows for certain the man can see into the future," said Chloe tying her hair back.

"So where do I come into all of this?" asked Isabella.

"I don't know. That's what we have to find out. All I know is that we will need the strength of the locket, the power you give it. I am certain of that!" said Lujzka.

"We must return to the main staff quarters," said Chloe suddenly, hearing a noise. "It's getting late and Spike Pennypinch will be sure to want to speak to you about work. He normally addresses everybody before lights out. He's a real task master, a truly unpleasant character."

They returned to find the other members of staff already gathered, looking tired and fed up. Isabella guessed there must be around a hundred people there in total. The noise of chatter died quickly as Spike burst into the room.

"Right!" he barked. "Firstly I have an announcement to make. I have just been informed by Madame Glittergold that the landlord and governor of Sumptitious, Mr Devin Fortuno is going to be gracing us with his presence the day after tomorrow – which means all days off are cancelled for the duration of his stay."

An angry wave of protesting voices rose up.

"That ain't right, Sir! I've been working three moonscapes solid now without a break!" shouted one middle aged woman bravely.

"Mrs Forbes. Do you ever stop whingeing?"

"As head housekeeper Sir, I feel I should speak up, not just fer meself, but fer some of the young 'uns too – we're all exhausted!" said Mrs Forbes defiantly, hands on her hips.

"You're workshy, that's your problem!" barked Spike.

"That ain't true, Sir. We all work very hard, from dawn to dusk, but we need to 'ave a break from time to time."

"Okay, you shall have a break…a permanent one – you're sacked! Get out of here!" snapped Spike.

"You can't do that, I've worked here for over twenty five years!" stammered the housekeeper.

"I can do as I damn well please – now get out before I kick your large backside onto the streets myself," he roared going red with rage.

A shocked hush filled the cold room, as the woman ran out sobbing into her apron.

Spike held up his hands. "Now listen to me you ungrateful rabble! Anybody unhappy with this arrangement can get out now…there are plenty of others to take your place, plenty of hungry mouths that need feeding in these difficult times. Well? Has anybody else got a complaint?"

The crowd shuffled around shaking their heads.

"Right then. As I was saying… Mr Fortuno will be accompanied by various guests including one extremely important gentleman. Madame Glittergold has told me to convey to you that under no circumstances are you to discuss this gentleman's stay here with anybody or you WILL be sacked on the spot! Under no circumstances are you to approach this gentleman unless he specifically summons you - or you WILL be sacked on the spot. You shall bow or curtsey when in his presence with your eyes cast down to the floor - or you WILL be sacked on the spot. I trust I make myself clear?"

"Yes, Sir," the staff muttered, all wondering who on earth this very important guest could be.

"The whole hotel will be emptied of current guests first thing after breakfast. You will all be ready for work before the suns are risen as there is much to be done before Mr Fortuno's arrival and I shall be inspecting all your work at regular intervals. If I find so much as a speck of dust, the person responsible for cleaning that area will be – guess what? Dismissed immediately! Right, off to bed then!" he barked, banging a nearby table.

"Not you two!" he said, pointing a finger at Lujzka and Isabella.

"Come here…and you too!" he shouted, beckoning over another girl with long dark hair. "You've worked here a while now – as a chambermaid under Mrs Forbes, I believe."

"Yes, Sir!"

"What's your name again?"

"Caoimhe, Sir," she said (pronouncing it as Quiva.)

"Right Miss Caoimhe, I am promoting you to the position of Head Housekeeper. These two are now your responsibility, and if they make any mistakes I will hold you accountable. You are to personally prepare the presidential suite for our honoured guest's arrival, as well as Mr Fortuno's private suite, plus you shall oversee the rest of the bedrooms for their entourages – understood?"

"Absolutely, Sir!" replied Caoimhe.

"Well what are you waiting for? Get to bed! The next few days are going to be very busy."

Chapter Twelve
LADY DEE AND LADY DAH

The following morning Caoimhe briefly explained to Isabella and Lujzka who everybody was. There was Mr Flusterfingers, the assistant manager, who was rushing around in his usual agitated manner, hands flailing and shouting orders at everybody. He was a gangly individual with wild, unkempt hair and was wearing a long tailed jacket that was clearly too tight around his midriff. His long suffering wife, Mrs Flusterfingers, was the hotel receptionist. She was busy chatting to a friend and trying to adjust a rather elaborate wig that was perched on her head.

Then there was Mr Moulder, who was extremely old and resembled a skeleton with wispy white hair. He was the doorman and rarely said a word to anybody. He shuffled around so slowly that it was hard to tell when he was moving.

"Who are those two?" asked Lujzka nodding her head towards the salon.

"Lady Dee and Lady Dah. They are cousins of Madame Glittergold," said Caoimhe in hushed tones. "They live here permanently. They're twin sisters. They think they're the bee's knees if you know what I mean - very snobbish."

The twins were sitting on a sofa, drinking tea. Lady Dee would take a sip and Lady Dah would swallow. It was a strange habit that they had, for example if one took a mouthful of food, the other would chew it - as if they were one and the same person. They would often finish off each other's sentences, as if they were telepathic. As one might expect with twins, they were almost identical in appearance with long oval faces and narrow noses. Their cheeks were high and well defined, their eyes large and hooded. Each was dressed elegantly - Lady Dee in a ruffled neck top and printed chiffon skirt, and Lady Dah in a lacy jacket and a black pair of wide trousers. Both had immaculately coiffed hair and wore formal hats – and it was clear that neither of them had ever done a day's work in their lives.

Lady Dah snapped her fingers at them. "Girl! Our teapot needs replenishing. Come on, we haven't all day!"

"Yes, we really are quite parched," Lady Dee added, dragging on a cigarette which her sister promptly exhaled through her heavily painted lips.

Caoimhe rolled her eyes and went over. "Look I'm responsible for housekeeping duties, not waitressing…"

"I don't care what you are responsible for!" said Lady Dah imperiously. "And I don't like the tone of your voice, girl!"

"What can I get for you?" said Caoimhe through gritted teeth, thinking of all the work she already had to do that day.

"Are you deaf, girl? My sister already told you!" snapped Lady Dee, "Tea! We need more tea!"

"Yes, girl and some of those little biscuits…oh but not those plain ones that you give to the riff-raff, we want those luxury chocolate ones," added Lady Dah, dismissing Caoimhe with a flick of her wrist.

"So my dear sister, what do you think Oro Cazador will be like? I hear he's very…"

"…wealthy. Yes, indeed. One of the richest men in Zartarbia and he's coming here – imagine that?!"

"Yes, imagine. I hear he's not much to look at but…"

"…who cares!"

They both giggled.

"Quite a catch by all accounts and apparently not married…"

"At the moment, sister dear, but that could all change…"

"You're quite right, indeed it might. I heard he may be the next owner of Sumptitious. Just imagine if he decided to marry one of us…we'd be wealthier than our cousin!"

"Yes, it would be Dorian's turn to grovel to us…she's so…"

"Stuck up! He might even give us this hotel as a wedding gift!"

"Who knows sister dear…but with our good looks..."

"How could he resist…?"

At that precise moment Spike Pennypinch walked past and overheard them.

"Why would somebody as powerful as Mr Cazador be remotely interested in two old maids like you. Let's face it - you're past your sell by dates! You're on the shelf and nobody in their right minds would want to marry either of you!" he said spitefully. "Besides I think you'll find it's Madame Glitttergold he's interested in, that's if she has anything to do with it."

"What do you mean by that you odious little man?" enquired Lady Dah sharply, narrowing her eyes at him.

Spike smiled a thin, twisted smile and tapped his nose. "That's for me to know and you to find out. But let's just say Madame has the upper hand."

"Get out of our sight you repellent moron and you can be sure Dorian shall hear about your impertinence towards us!" hissed Lady Dah.

Spike laughed humourlessly. "Like she will care. Just remember you only have a roof over your heads because of Madame's good grace. I'm sure a few choice words in her ear could change that state of affairs."

"We are her family...whilst you're nothing more than a common servant!"

"Servant maybe, but valuable definitely. I run Hotel Gastronomic and this place would fall apart if it wasn't for me and Madame Glittergold knows it. Believe me when I say, if she had to make a choice it would be your suitcases in the gutter...not mine."

He turned abruptly leaving the two sisters fuming.

"The coarseness of that man!" spluttered Lady Dee.

"Indeed, nothing more than an ignorant, jumped up bumpkin!" blustered Lady Dah. "We really must do something about him sister dear!"

"I agree...but what?"

"I don't know but we'll think of a plan, you rest assured."

Caoimhe returned with a tray of fresh tea and biscuits. She set it down on the table and began to unload it.

"Well, this really is not good enough girl!" snapped Lady Dah.

"What is the problem?" asked Caoimhe sighing.

"There is no doily on the biscuit plate..."

"...and this teaspoon has not been polished! I should be able to see my reflection in it!"

"Yes, quite so and this tea is too strong! Mr Flusterfingers! Mr Flusterfingers!" Lady Dah shrieked across the salon.

The assistant manager ran over, wringing his hands. "What's the matter now?"

"It's her!" said Lady Dee pointing a finger at Caoimhe. "She's an imbecile!"

"Quite so, you really must do something about her, in fact all the staff around here! You need to train them properly!" sneered Lady Dah.

"Now get us some more tea, something that doesn't look as if it has been sitting in the pot for several days…and clean teaspoons!" said Lady Dee haughtily.

Mr Flusterfingers pursed his lips and said. "Is there anything else your ladyships require?"

"I don't like the tone of your voice."

"Perhaps the shirt off my back?" he continued.

"Well really, we're not going to sit here…" began Lady Dee.

"…and be insulted!" finished Lady Dah.

"Then perhaps you would care to stand up and be insulted!" retorted Mr Flusterfingers glowering at them.

Caoimhe had to stifle a giggle as both sisters went quite red in the face.

"In case you hadn't noticed, we have an important guest arriving tomorrow and I don't think Madame Glittergold will be pleased if she finds out things are not ready because of your petty complaints! Caoimhe, I need you to take the two new girls to go and check the rooms for Mr Cazador and his guests. Now then, some of us have work to do," he turned back to the sisters, "so if you have any further complaints, then I suggest you stick them where the sun doesn't shine!"

Chapter Thirteen
PREPARATIONS ARE MADE

"What happened?" asked Isabella as Caoimhe returned to them. "Nothing to worry about. They're always like that, though it was funny to see the looks on their faces when Mr Flusterfingers told them off. Anyway we need to get on with preparing the presidential suite. Come with me."

She led them up the enormous staircase and into an old fashioned elevator that was situated in a separate wing of the hotel. She slid back the metal grid door and they all stepped in, going up for what seemed an eternity. Finally they reached the top floor and headed towards the presidential suite.

Isabella could not help but gasp when she saw the rooms. It was more like a separate house decorated to the most luxurious standards.

Firstly there was a reception room where two stone lion fountains greeted them, spouting champagne from their mouths. They then walked through to the master bedroom, where an ornate bed hung from the ceiling. It was big enough to fit four people into it comfortably and was fringed with tassels made from spun gold and saffron. The pillows were stuffed with the sweetest smelling spices and the covers were woven from the softest feathers plucked from the most exotic birds.

The bathroom (if you could call it that) was like entering the most stunning private beach you have ever seen. The floor was coated with white sand as fine as powder. Palm trees stood in each corner and the bath was in fact a large pool full of fresh rose petals, which had a waterfall cascading into it. If you so wished, you could bathe in hot chocolate or frothy milkshakes rather than water, and the bathrobes were made from jasmine blossoms.

The sink was decorated with mother of pearl shells and the toilet was discreetly concealed behind a curtain of tiger lilies. The walls were digital screens that depicted various sunsets or sunrises that could be changed to suit your mood.

"Right, Lujzka if you could make a start in here. You need to rake the sand, polish the palm leaves and check down this list to make sure that nothing is missing. You will find additional toiletries in here," she said pressing a rock next to the bath, which opened to reveal a cupboard full of expensive perfumes and soaps.

"Isabella, you can help me in the other bedrooms."

As soon as she was by herself, Lujzka quickly began to conceal the FADF bugging devices. They were only the size of pinheads, so it wasn't too difficult but she knew that every room would be scanned, so she also planted some larger fake ones in slightly more obvious places too.

To get to the other adjoining bedrooms, the girls had to pass through a roof top terrace that led to a large lake. Upon arriving at the lake you could see there were three beautiful boats moored, each with a security guard in attendance, who pulled the vessels in as soon as they saw Caoimhe.

She stepped nimbly aboard the first, then turned to help Isabella.

Mr and Mrs Fluster-fingers

Inside the boat there was another bedroom and bathroom, and the walls were studded with brilliant jewels and delicious sweets. Inside the second boat, the theme was dark chocolate with furniture intricately carved from it and studded with sugar almonds, and on boat three there was a shell bed covered with a tent of spun sugar.

"Wow!" said Isabella, looking around in wonderment. "Where did they get all this stuff from?"

Caoimhe shrugged. "I suppose Malveo made the edible things. He's the chef here…or at least that's what Madame Glittergold claims but, if you ask me, he spends so much time eating, I don't know where he finds the time to do any cooking," she murmured in a dismissive tone.

"He must be really clever."

"You obviously haven't met him yet," said Caoimhe dryly, handing her some cleaning equipment. "You start with the windows and make sure there are no smudges or Mr Pennypinch will have my guts for garters! And I can't afford to lose my job like poor old Mrs Forbes."

"Yes he does seem a bit harsh," said Isabella as she began polishing the glass panes. "So what's he like then, this Malveo guy?"

"A bit of a twit really, but the food that comes out of that kitchen is quite something else, I'll give him that…mind you he's ever so secretive. Nobody except him, his mother and Mr Pennypinch are allowed into the kitchen which, if you ask me, is a bit odd."

"Yes, I suppose it is a little strange. So how do the waiters get the food for the customers?"

"It comes out on this conveyer belt thing… in the pantry area."

"Where's that then?"

"You're asking a lot of questions and look, you've missed a bit there. That's what comes of talking too much and not paying attention!" said Caoimhe sharply pointing at the offending smudge. "Sorry I don't mean to snap at you, I know it's your first day and everything but I need this job, I have to support my parents," she said softening her tone.

"It's alright. I'll do it again," said Isabella, wondering how Lujzka was getting on.

Meanwhile, in the kitchen…

"So you understand what you have to do?" hissed Dorian Glittergold, grabbing Isaac by his ear.

"Yes," he winced. "You want me to create a potion that will make the person who drinks it, to fall in love with the first person they set eyes on."

"Correct. And what will it taste of?"

"Nothing. Whoever drinks it won't realise if it is added to another stronger tasting liquid."

"How do you know the brat won't try to trick you Madame?" said Spike warming his back against the dying embers of the kitchen fire.

Dorian Glittergold pursed her lips and smiled nastily. "Oh he wouldn't dare trick me…would you? Because he knows what will happen to him!"

She pinched Isaac's gaunt cheeks hard.

"Oooww!" shrieked the child. "I promise I wouldn't trick you stepmother!"

"Don't call me that! How many times have I told you! If you wish to address me you call me ma'am…or maybe I should get Mr Pennypinch here to beat it into your memory…"

"It would be a pleasure. Discipline is what he needs!" Spike said unbuckling his belt. "And plenty of it!"

"That won't be necessary at the moment Mr Pennypinch. I think he understands how much work he has for the next few days and how important it is that he gets it right!" she said twisting his ear spitefully, "Now, you will do as you are told or I will punish you severely. Do I make myself understood? Otherwise I'll feed you to the dogs."

Isaac nodded miserably and scuttled over to a cupboard and began to take out various potions and powders.

"I shall start now ma'am...you won't be disappointed..." he stammered, his large eyes blinking nervously.

"Have the menu for tomorrow's feast ready for me first thing in the morning and, you snivelling excuse of a creature, remember it better be good! If my guest is displeased in any way whatsoever..." Madame Glittergold let her sentence hang in the air unfinished so that Isaac could only imagine what awful punishments she would devise.

She stood hands on hips, her face like a monstrous waxwork in the flickering light. "Come Mr Pennypinch, let us retire for a night cap. We have much to discuss before Mr Cazador's arrival."

She turned, her high-heeled shoes striking the stone floor like flints as she left the kitchen.

Spike Pennypinch grinned unpleasantly at the boy, drawing his finger across his throat. "You're time's running out, little rat," he whispered, and with that he left, locking the door behind him.

Chapter Fourteen
THE ARRIVAL OF ORO CAZADOR

The day of Oro Cazador's arrival dawned and The Hotel Gastronomic was in a state of hysterical activity. Mr Flusterfingers was busy shooing out the last remaining guests.

"But we are booked in for three nights!" complained one disgruntled gentleman. "I booked it a year ago, and my wife has been looking forward to coming here for ages. This really is most unacceptable!!!"

"Can't be helped," said Mr Flusterfingers rudely pushing him out of the door. "Now off you go, I can't have you cluttering up the entrance!"

"How dare you! I really must protest. I am not satisfied with this treatment!" blustered the gentleman, going red in the face.

"Well, riff-raff like you never are!" said the assistant manager, slamming the door in his face and going to check that the staff were working hard.

Slowly the hotel was transformed - the carpets were hoovered five times, the crystal glasses polished and re-polished, the air sprayed with the most fragrant of scents. Above all, a new range of furniture had been created especially to the highest standards -

everything edible and utterly delicious. Chairs had been made from freshly baked bread and were upholstered with smoked salmon cushions; sofas constructed from iced biscuits and fondant; shaggy rugs woven from mixed lettuce leaves.

Dorian Glittergold was busy checking the flower arrangements with the hotel gardener, Orlando.

"I said I wanted yellow roses…not cream. If I wanted cream I would have specially asked for cream, but I clearly told you yellow!" she shouted at the unfortunate gardener.

"I'm sorry Madame Glittergold, but the yellow ones aren't in bloom yet," he said trying to explain. "If I had had more warning…"

"More warning? I'll give you a warning! Get these changed or you're fired!"

"Yes Madame Glittergold…but where from?"

"I don't care! Just make sure it's done otherwise you and your grandfather are out on the streets!"

"But he's an invalid!"

"That's your problem! Now, you stay in MY staff accommodation, I pay YOUR wages and you WILL do as you're told, so GET IT SORTED OUT!!!" she screamed turning to her two cousins. "Really! The boy is an imbecile! Must I oversee every detail?"

"Poor dear," said Lady Dee filing her nails. "It's always the same with servants, give them an inch and they take a mile! Mind you, I thought that manager – what's his name again?"

"Oh that ghastly man, Pennypinch…" her sister intervened, pulling a face.

"Yes that's it! I thought that was his job, to oversee things cousin dear, so that you did not have to exert yourself unduly…really if I were you I should be quite minded to replace him…"

HOTEL
GASTRONOMIC

MR. MOULDER

Mr Moulder
the Head Doorman

"…He clearly isn't up to the high standards you expect," finished Lady Dah.

"I am fully aware of your dislike of Mr Pennypinch, but this is my hotel – not yours!" glowered Madame Glittergold as she rubbed her forehead.

"Oh course cousin dear…" soothed Lady Dee, "We weren't inferring anything about your choice of servant."

"…we only have your best interests at heart," cooed Lady Dah.

"Yes, cousin dearest and you look quite fatigued. Why don't you sit down…"

"…and have a nice cup of tea?" joined in Lady Dah patting the cushion next to her.

"Well maybe just for a moment I do feel rather exhausted," said Madame Glittergold flopping her large bottom onto the seat. "There's just so much to do and I want everything to be perfect."

"Of course you do," cooed Lady Dee, as she admired her manicured hands. "You're a perfectionist and the servants are just bone idle! Really if they knew…"

"…the pressure they put you under!" said Lady Dah.

"Yes, we just want to make sure that people like that Pennypinch fellow don't take advantage of you…" Lady Dee urged.

"…and your good nature," finished Lady Dah.

"I couldn't agree more, sister dear," Lady Dee nodded. "You've worked your fingers to the bone to make this hotel the success it is today…"

"…and that lout of a manager takes all the credit!" said Lady Dah, massaging Dorian's shoulders. "Goodness me aren't you tense!"

This was, in fact, an enormous lie because Dorian Glittergold was the laziest person you would ever have the misfortune to meet. Her day comprised of getting up at noon and having a gigantic breakfast, taking a leisurely bath and squeezing herself into one of zillions of extravagant outfits (all far too small for her as she refused to acknowledge she was hopelessly overweight). Whenever her costumier, Herr Higglepiggle, would come to visit to take her measurements for her latest dress, he would always have to lie as she would throw a total temper tantrum if he dared to suggest she was not the size she said she was.

(Now don't get me wrong, there are plenty of people who are overweight due to health problems or big bones, but Dorian was not one of these people. She and her son, Malveo, were grossly obese because they ate far too much of the wrong types of food and never, *ever* did they exercise).

Having prepared herself for the day, Dorian would emerge from her room and spend the day shouting at the long-suffering staff she employed at The Hotel Gastronomic. As it was so difficult to find work in Sumptitious, the employees would put up with her cantankerous ways – they had no choice as it was that or starve. In-between shouting at her staff, she would pause to take tea with Lady Dee and Dah, who were both great at sucking up to their wealthy relative. Although they despised her like everyone else, they were wholly dependant on her from a financial point of view and were not about to jeopardise that.

After being flattered to the point of boredom by her cousins, Dorian generally poured herself several glasses of expensive champagne and curled up on a sofa with Malveo and Tootles to watch various chat shows. Alternatively they would go to the kitchen to bully Isaac, for they were positively foul people who did not have a nice bone in their bodies! (Now I know this all seems very unfair but it is usually the way that those who do wrong will ultimately pay the price because, luckily, there are more good people than bad in the world).

"Now my dear, why don't you go and have a nice long soak in the bath. After all you want to make a good impression on Mr Cazador," said Lady Dee, thinking privately that no amount of pampering would ever make her cousin look attractive.

"What are you going to wear?" asked Lady Dah.

"Herr Higglepiggle is due any moment now," said Dorian looking at her watch. "He's bringing a selection of gowns for me to choose from."

"I'm sure they will be most delightful!"

"Yes, the man has such exquisite taste!" gushed Lady Dah, knowing full well that her cousin had the most appalling dress sense. "Mind you, make sure he doesn't try to dress you in anything too showy!" she added patting her cousin's plump hand.

"Yes after all men like a little mystery, they don't want all the goods on display," said Lady Dee raising an arched eyebrow.

"Though I'm sure whatever you wear will be utterly enchanting," said Lady Dah unconvincingly.

"She's right. Mystery and elegance – the ultimate way to trap your man," tittered her sister.

"Well between you and me…I have been reliably informed Mr Cazador is ready to enjoy the comfort a lady could bring into his lonely life," murmured Dorian.

"Is that so?" the sisters said in mock surprise. "How thrilling!"

"Don't be getting any ideas! He's mine. I don't want either of you even *thinking* about making a play for him – Mr Pennypinch told me that you might be harbouring expectations above your station," she said sharply.

"I've told you cousin dear, the man is a feckless lout. He is trying to drive a wedge between us. We only want what is best for your happiness," said Lady Dah feigning distress. "I don't know how you could say such a thing!"

"Yes, we only want what is best for you and I'm sure you will get what you deserve," added Lady Dee, trying to look suitably perturbed.

"Oh, I know I will…I have a little something up my sleeve," said Dorian knowingly.

"You have a plan, oh do tell?" chorused the twins.

"Let's just say I am confident that the odds are going to be in my favour where the attentions of Mr Cazador are concerned," said Dorian Glittergold patting her hair. "Anyway, I really can't sit around chatting. I must go and get ready."

"What's she up to?" hissed Lady Dah to her sister after Dorian had departed.

"I don't know," said Lady Dee biting into a biscuit, "but you know how ruthless she is once she sets her mind to it!"

Lady Dah chewed the biscuit and swallowed. "I don't trust her!"

"Well that goes without saying. We must be careful."

It was late afternoon and the suns had cast a golden syrup light over the land. In the distance, a convoy of elephants and horses could be seen flying through the dust of the sunset, pulling numerous carriages and coaches behind them.

The animals were each decorated with bright paintings upon their bodies and were adorned with elaborate cloaks. The carriages glittered and shimmered as they flew above the clouds. Oro Cazador and his entourage had almost reached their destination.

"They're here! They're here! Come on everybody! Into place, quick sharp!" shouted Mr Flusterfingers, leaping around like a thing possessed, his hands flaying left, right and centre. "Everybody in line…we want to make a good impression. This is the most important guest we have had after all, the kind of client that will put us firmly on the map of Zartarbia. You! Go and open the doors!" he said, jabbing a finger at Mr Moulder, the doorman. "Hurry up, you old fossil!" he shouted at the elderly man. "I swear I've seen more life in a graveyard!"

A few moments later Oro Cazador swept through the door followed closely by Glace, Lily, Betrug Espion and various other members of his extensive staff.

"Welcome, welcome, one and all! Mr Cazador obviously we've been expecting you. Allow me to introduce myself - I am Mr Flusterfingers, assistant manager of the Hotel Gastronomic. Let me say what an honour… what a privilege… it is to have you staying as a guest. If there is anything we can do, you need only ask," he bowed low with an elaborate flourish.

Oro ignored him, walking past the lined up employees. Mr Flusterfingers quickly straightened up and hurried after him. "Yes, of course you must be tired after your long journey. I'll show you straight to your rooms and arrange refreshments for you…" he gushed, tripping over himself and landing flat on his face.

"Flusterfingers…I shall deal with this!" barked Spike Pennypinch marching over. "You must excuse my colleague's over-enthusiasm." "We are honoured by your presence, Sir," said Spike holding out his hand. "I am Mr Pennypinch, manager of this wondrous hotel…"

"Where is the proprietor?" said Oro curtly, taking off his gloves and giving them to Spike rather than shaking his hand.

"Madame Glittergold…oh yes…I shall inform her of your arrival immediately…" he snapped his fingers at Mr Flusterfingers. "Let Madame know that our guests are here!"

"No need," said Dorian Glittergold standing at the top of the stairs, dressed in a most outrageous outfit. She wore a long flowing gown that revealed far too much of her ample cleavage. It was made from spun caramel and crystallized violets, with the hemline and cuffs trimmed with cup cakes and French fancies. On her head was perched a hat made from a raspberry cream tartlet and her shoes were made from fudge.

"I'm afraid pressing business delayed me somewhat Mr Cazador," she said as she walked down the giant staircase accompanied by Malveo, Tootles and her cousins.

She teetered across the marble floor in her high-heeled shoes and breathlessly introduced herself to Oro, proffering a chubby hand for him to kiss.

"My dear lady, what a pleasure to finally meet you. Mr Fortuno has told me so much about you and your delightful hotel," said Oro, turning the spotlight of his charm onto her.

Dorian fluttered her false eyelashes and attempted a coy smile that looked quite grotesque under the thick layer of make up she was wearing.

"I can assure you Mr Cazador, the pleasure is all mine and please, call me Dorian. This is my darling son Malveo, who I might add is also the talented chef behind our humble success," she said pulling him forward. "Go on pumpkin, say hello."

Lady Dee and Lady Dah raised their eyebrows simultaneously as Malveo (who had been picking his nose) held out his hand for Oro to shake.

"Delighted, Master Glittergold," said Oro bowing instead, trying to mask his disgust at the boy's behaviour. Dorian elbowed her son in the ribs, indicating he should do the same.

Lady Dee and Lady Dah cleared their throats to draw attention to themselves.

"And who are these two divine creatures Madame Glittergold? You haven't introduced me to them yet!"

"Oh they're just my cousins," said Dorian patting each of them on their arms. "After my poor late husband died well, I was struggling with my grief – you understand. I am not a woman who is used to being alone." She fluttered her eye lashes again. "Well my dear cousins had fallen on hard times, they had nowhere to live, so I invited them to stay here as my…companions."

Lady Dee and Lady Dah smiled through clenched teeth, hating their cousin's patronising attitude.

"My goodness I am surrounded by beautiful women!"

Tootles the pig grunted and pulled against the blue ribbon lead that was tied around his neck straining to eat the cake trim of Madame Glittergold's dress.

"Oh! Naughty boy!" she said indulgently picking the pig up. "This is my precious Tootles. Say hello to Mr Cazador," she added waggling one of his trotters in an embarrassing parody of a wave.

"Well I see you have already met Mr Spike Pennypinch – general manager of our little hotel," she continued.

"Mr Cazador, welcome again," said Spike nodding his head in acknowledgement. "I hope you and your guests will enjoy your stay with us. A banquet has been arranged in your honour for this evening."

"How thoughtful of you," he said, addressing his reply to Dorian, "though I am not sure of the exact time that my associate Mr Devin Fortuno is arriving."

"Oh, don't worry. Mr Fortuno has already contacted me to let me know that he and his good lady wife will be with us in time for the dinner. He said he wouldn't miss it for the world!" gushed Dorian.

"Is that so?" said Cazador, as he turned to his daughter, urging her to step forward. Lily stepped forward shyly, daunted by Dorian's magnificent ugliness. "Allow me to introduce my daughter, Lily Rose." His daughter smiled awkwardly, reluctantly putting her hand forward.

"How beautiful, quite the china doll! My goodness what an enchanting child! Like father like daughter," Dorian said effusively, seizing Lily's delicate, white hand.

"My sister Glace," continued Oro.

"Delighted I'm sure," oozed Dorian. Glace smiled thinly before turning her head away.

"…and my bodyguard Mr Espion."

Betrug gave a small, curt bow, watching Dorian Glittergold with his cold slanted eyes. His face gave nothing away, a blank canvas devoid of emotion. Dorian smiled uncertainly, feeling quite unnerved by the Transcender's presence.

"He will be overseeing all security arrangements, I hope this will not inconvenience you too much dear lady but unfortunately it is an essential precaution."

"I understand…a man of your position can't be too careful. Mr Pennypinch will assist you in any way he can."

"I will need to check the guest rooms first," said Betrug brusquely.

"Yes of course, please, follow me, and I shall personally show you to your rooms," said Dorian. "Mr Flusterfingers, I shall leave you to look after Mr Cazador's entourage."

"Of course Madame Glittergold," said the assistant manager rubbing his hands together. "Your wish is my command."

He watched her go upstairs and then turned to the waiting group of personal secretaries, butlers, hairdressers, maids and manicurists. "Staff quarters are situated in the basement," he said pompously, pointing to a dingy stairwell. "Don't expect any special treatment – that is reserved for your master."

Dorian led Oro to the presidential suite. "I hope everything is to your satisfaction. This is the best room in my hotel but obviously if there is anything I can do to make your stay more comfortable, you must let me know," she said flirtatiously, giving him a knowing look.

"My dear lady, your generous hospitality is overwhelming," said Oro smiling his most endearing smile. "If you don't mind I would like to freshen up but I greatly look forward to enjoying your delightful company this evening and, if I may be so bold…getting better acquainted with you."

He took her hand and pressed a lingering kiss onto it. Dorian tittered and blushed a deeply unattractive shade of crimson.

"Mr Cazador, I also look forward to getting to know you better. It is rare indeed that I get the opportunity to meet such a gentleman as yourself. There are so few…well…cultured men around."

"I find that surprising, such a fine woman as yourself…I would imagine that you have no shortage of suitors," said Oro stroking his moustache.

"You're too kind Mr Cazador."

"Dorian, my dear lady - you really must call me Oro, I insist…now if you will excuse me, it has been a tiring journey."

"Of course. Mr Cazador…I mean Oro. Well, until tonight," she simpered, waving goodbye girlishly.

The moment Dorian had departed, Oro's attitude changed immediately.

"Betrug check the room for bugs or any other spy devices," he growled. "Lauren! Take my daughter to her quarters. You and you!" he said snapping his fingers at two bodyguards. "Accompany them!"

A steady stream of servants carried in vast quantities of trunks and cases, and immediately began unpacking the luggage as Oro went to the balcony with his sister. "What a vile old hag!" he spat out in disgust. "Fortuno had better be right about this."

"She really is quite odious," agreed Glace, "but bide your time brother."

Betrug appeared behind them. "Sir, the rooms are clear now. There were a few standard bugs but that seems to be all," he said holding the devices in his hand.

"So what now?" he said.

"We wait until this evening," said Oro gruffly.

Chapter Fifteen
THE SECRET MEETING

Lily Rose went out onto the huge terrace with Lauren, the two bodyguards following closely behind them.

Lily tipped her face up towards the sky. "How good it is to feel fresh air on my face."

"It is lovely here mi'lady," agreed Lauren.

"Look at the gardens here," she said wistfully. "They are so beautiful."

"Who's that down there?" said Lauren shielding her eyes.

"Where?"

"Look just there, by that tall tree."

A handsome young man emerged from the shadows, clearly looking up at them. He smiled and waved. Lily checked over her shoulder to check whether the bodyguards had noticed him but they were busy in conversation.

Suddenly a tiny bird landed on the wall surrounding the balcony. In its beak was a folded piece of paper. The two girls looked at each other, before Lily quickly took the letter from the bird and opened it:

'I hope you don't think I am being too forward but I saw you arrive with your father and I just wanted to say I think you are the

most beautiful girl I have ever seen. I would like to know you name.
Mine is Orlando, I am the gardener here. I wondered if you liked
flowers, and whether you might allow me to escort you around the
gardens – obviously with your father's permission'

"What does it say?" whispered Lauren.

Lily handed it to her. "Do you think I should reply?"

The bird cocked its head to one side and chirped.

"Your father would be furious," said Lauren nervously.

"But he is rather good looking," giggled Lily. "Why shouldn't I
have a friend?"

"You know why…it's too dangerous!"

"Quick give me a pen!" urged Lily, and she quickly scribbled
on the back of the paper before folding it back up and holding it
towards the little bird to take in his beak. The bird seemed for a
moment to wink at her, before spreading its wings and swooping
back down to Orlando.

"Lily! What are you up to?" her father's voice boomed across
the courtyard. "Are you ready for dinner yet?"

The girls turned around, trying not to look guilty as the
bodyguards spun around and marched over to them.

"No Papa, I will go and change now. Lauren was just reminding
me, but I was just so enjoying the view…and Papa, I just wanted
to say thank you for letting me accompany you on this trip!" she
ran over to her father hugging him. "It's the best present you have
ever given me!"

"Well, I am glad you are in a better humour," said Oro gruffly,
secretly delighted by his daughter's change of heart.

Spike Pennypinch was checking the last minute arrangements for
the evening's dinner in The Great Hall. He was bossing everybody
around as usual and the room was frenetic with activity.

"Flusterfingers!" he shouted. "Come here now!"

The assistant manager rolled his eyes and hastened over to where Pennypinch stood. "Mr Pennypinch, what is the problem?"

"I told you I wanted the napkins folded in the shape of swans not fans! I also gave you specific instructions to use the mother of pearl place mats . Change them immediately! I'm going to the kitchen to check on the food."

"But I thought you said…"

"Just do as I say! Remember, tonight has to be perfect…attention to detail at all times!"

"Yes, of course sir!" he said through gritted teeth as he nodded a bow to his superior.

Lujzka waited until they had walked away before turning to the waitress nearest her.

"How long have we got?" she said in a low voice.

"The banquet is due to start in around three hours."

"Can you cover for me for a few minutes?"

"I don't know…I've just been promoted," the waitress hesitated. "What are you up to?"

"Nothing…I suddenly remembered Madame Glittergold asked me to tell one of the other girls that she was meant to be organising a special surprise for the VIP…I forgot and I don't want to get her into trouble."

"Okay, but please just hurry back!"

Lujzka quickly ran past The Library, through reception and to the cloakroom where she had arranged to meet Chloe. She looked either way to make sure she had not been followed before pulling back the curtain and stepping into the dimly lit space. Rows and rows of coats lined the room, and carefully Lujzka pushed through them.

"Hello…," she called out quietly. "It's me, Lujzka!"

There was a faint shuffling sound, fabric twitching and then silence again.

"Is anybody there?"

She moved cautiously, further into the darkness.

"Is anybody there?" she repeated.

Suddenly a figure stepped out blocking her path.

"You startled me Chloe!" Lujzka said.

"Sorry."

"Listen I don't have much time…I've got to be back in the Great Hall as soon as possible…firstly the operational code…we can't be too careful," said Lujzka.

"Yes, of course… 263AD89…" Chloe supplied the necessary code.

"His spies are everywhere," said Lujzka, looking around. "Do you know if the decoy bugging devices I planted in Cazador's room were found?"

"Yes, they were."

"By Espion I presume?"

"Yes," nodded Chloe.

"Good. Then they won't be suspicious and start searching for the real ones. Now listen, I have some more. Can you conceal them in Devin Fortuno's private quarters…I overheard Mrs Flusterfingers telling her husband he wasn't due to arrive until early evening, so you have time, but be careful. The amount of security Cazador surrounds himself with makes our task difficult and Espion is watching everyone, which is why he is less likely to suspect you rather than me. He will look to any newcomers first, so I have to be careful not to draw attention to myself."

"Leave Betrug Espion to me…I've been watching his movements. Anyway, what have you found out?" said Chloe.

"Not much, but we should know more by this evening…this is a delicate operation and we can't jeopardise our positions here."

"Do you want me to do anything else?"

"Yes, get this message to FADF head quarters – I've coded it as a precaution but Cazador is intelligent as well as paranoid, so remember to take it underground somewhere so that he won't be able to track it," she handed Chloe a folded holographic telegram. "Make sure no one sees you – I don't think I need to remind you of the consequences if this information falls into the wrong hands…"

"Don't worry, there's a cellar here, I'll send it from there. What does it say?" said Chloe.

"Just what we all discussed earlier."

"We'd both best get back," said Chloe, "before our absence is noticed."

Lujzka nodded. "Report to me by first dawn tomorrow morning…no contact before then, unless it is an emergency…and good luck."

"Understood," said Chloe smiling. "You had better go first and I will follow a few moments later – I shall see you at the banquet."

"Yes, it should be interesting."

Lujzka left as quietly as she had come.

Chloe waited until she had heard the FADF agent's footsteps melt into silence. As she looked at the folded hologram, her features began to metamorphose into something quite different. Her skin was sucked back inside her head until it was replaced with the face of Betrug Espion.

His mouth twisted into a vicious smile as he unfolded the hologram.

"No we wouldn't want this getting into the wrong hands," he said to himself. "So, the FADF think they can infiltrate our operation? More fools them to underestimate the stealth of a

Transcender. Now I have one spy, and the trap is laid for the other…it's a good thing I was able to get the code out of her."

He quickly placed the message into his jacket pocket, patting it happily. "Mr Cazador will be most pleased."

Betrug pulled back the curtains of the cloakroom just as a breathless Isabella was about to enter. She glanced up at him, a look of panic crossing her face.

"Are you looking for somebody?" he asked, the tone of his voice quietly sinister as he stood towering above her

"No…er, no…I just had to fetch a coat for one of the guests…" she stammered, thinking of the first excuse that came into her head.

"Well you don't want to keep them waiting do you?" said Betrug, stepping aside for her to enter the cloakroom. "Don't let me stop you."

Something instinctively told her that she was in danger and she knew to listen to her instincts. "Oh! I forgot the gentleman's ticket…I will never find his jacket without it…I had best go and fetch it."

Betrug smiled at her coldly. "Run along then little girl…it's getting late…and dark…"

Isabella needed no further warning. She ran as fast as she could away from him.

Chapter Sixteen
A FEAST FIT FOR A KING

Spike Pennypinch walked down the long corridor leading to the kitchen and removed a large key from around his neck to open the door. The heavy sound of wood dragging against the stone floor alerted Isaac who was busy preparing the gourmet feast for the evening.

"Mr Pennypinch, Sir…I…I wasn't expecting you until later. I presume you have come to check on the preparations, Sir."

"Don't presume anything! You're not clever enough!" snarled Spike, slamming the door behind him.

"What's *he* doing in here?" he added, pointing at Malveo who was busy sticking his podgy fingers into various pots and pans.

"Please…I…I…I have tried asking him to leave…" Isaac stammered, turning to his stepbrother, "…oh please don't do that, you'll spoil the balance of ingredients. "

"Who cares what you think?" grunted Malveo, spluttering cake crumbs from his rubbery lips. "This is delicious…I could eat the whole lot!"

"Get your fat face out of those Malveo!" barked Spike, marching over and cuffing him round the ear.

"Ouch! What did you do that for!"

"Get out of the kitchen now!"

"But I'm hungry and mother said I had to stay in here until she called for me," Malveo said stubbornly, wiping a smear of chocolate from his face.

"You'll explode one day with the amount of food you stuff your face with," snorted Spike, truly despising the heir to the Gastronomic empire. Spike ensured he took every opportunity to discredit Malveo in the vague hope that one day it might be him, not Malveo, that inherited the hotel.

"I'm going to tell mummy that you're being horrid to me," replied Malveo, defiantly stuffing a large roast potato into his greedy mouth.

Spike shot him a filthy look. "Just do as you're told. If this evening doesn't go according to plan…"

"Then what? It will be your job on the line," Malveo grinned evilly.

Spike raised an eyebrow and hissed. "You'd do best to remember that your mother wants to impress Mr Cazador and if that doesn't happen, she will blame you not me – particularly when I tell her that you meddled in the kitchen and ruined the recipes!"

"You're just a nasty person! Don't think my mother doesn't know that. She'll be furious when she hears what you've said to me!" said Malveo, backing off slightly.

"Oh no!" said Spike throwing his hands in the air in mock horror. "Please don't call me nasty…oh anything than that!"

He lowered his voice suddenly to an ice cold whisper. "Believe me, the feeling is mutual. Now get out and keep yourself hidden. Come back at precisely 8pm to make your grand appearance – as the Secret Chef! Ha! That's a joke!!" He grabbed the boy by the scruff of his neck and frogmarched him out of the kitchen, slamming the door in his face before turning his attention to Isaac. He cast his eye over the feast that lay before him and despite himself he could not help but salivate, "Is this exactly as instructed?"

"Yes sir...Madame Glittergold approved the menu this morning..." trembled the child.

"Well don't stop working on my account; I'm sure you've still got plenty to do."

Spike picked up the menu, reading through the list of delicious dishes.

Spike picked up a canapé shaped like a wrapped sweetie and popped it into his mouth. Immediately he felt the flavours melting, blending, running down the back of his throat. It was a delicious cascade of tastes that made him feel as if he was the most important person in the whole of Zartarbia. He picked up another and gobbled it up, unable to help himself, such was the addictive quality of the food. Isaac watched him nervously out of the corner of his eye.

"What? What are you staring at?"

"Nothing Sir," replied Isaac, trying to concentrate on the sauce he was stirring.

"It's a big night for you, isn't it? Your mother and father must be so proud of their precious - clever – beloved son..." Spike said sarcastically picking up another canapé. The child didn't reply but inside his heart lurched, understanding the vindictive tone in Spike's voice.

"I didn't hear your answer," Spike goaded. "I said your parents must be so proud of you. What's the matter? Cat got your tongue?"

"You know they're dead," said Isaac quietly, lowering his eyes.

"Oh yes, poor pathetic orphan... no one to care for you now...no one to miss you and certainly nobody to love you..." Spike crooned.

The Hotel Gastronomic
Banquet Menu in Honour of Mr. Oro Cazador

Canapés

Bon bons of tiger prawns and avocado puree wrapped in transparent rice pastry and tartlets of quail and pear.

Starter

A sliver of toasted venison and pheasant terrine topped with the finest caviar and served with a delicious apricot sauce.

Interlude

Lollypops of watermelon and champagne sorbet served with a twist of cured ham and fresh mint.

Main Course

Beef and oyster pie served with baby new potatoes and curled bacon vases filled with fresh vegetables.

Dessert

White chocolate carved in the shape of a swan decorated with forest fruits and crystallized primroses and violets.

Cheese and Biscuits

"Leave me alone!" Isaac suddenly snapped.

"You're nothing but a worthless little freak. You've got no one and nothing and it's all you deserve!" he said advancing on the cowering child.

"Get away from me!"

At that moment Dorian Glittergold entered the kitchen.

"What's going on?" she demanded coldly.

Spike straightened up and moved away from Isaac. "Nothing Madame, the little idiot was back chatting me, that's all. You know how he is…I was about to discipline him…"

Dorian held up a gloved hand, "Not now Spike...he has to finish the preparations for this evening."

"As you wish, Madame."

"Go and check if Mr Cazador and his guests have everything they need before dinner. Tell them champagne will be served at 7pm in the Library and make sure everything is perfect. Nothing must spoil my plans."

Spike nodded and left the room.

"Now, where is the potion I instructed you to concoct for me?" she demanded, "Give it to me now!"

Isaac hurriedly pulled a small bottle from his pocket and handed it to her.

Her piggy eyes lit up, as she unstoppered it and sniffing the contents asked, "Are you sure this will work?"

"Yes," said Isaac, his huge eyes blinking.

"And you are positive that it will make the recipient fall in love with the first person they lay eyes on?"

Isaac nodded.

"If you are lying…if this is a trick…" she hissed, "make no mistake, if just one single thing goes wrong I will make you sorry that you were born. Now get on. We shall be eating at 8pm precisely – understood?"

Oro Cazador and
Madame
Glittergold
at the
Hotel

Isaac nodded miserably.

"Right. Well, what are you gawping at? Finish up your work!" she said as she slammed the door behind her.

Drinks were duly served in the Library that evening for Oro Cazador and his entourage; Devin Fortuno and his wife Opal Luvie had finally arrived early evening and now everyone was assembled together. Dorian had given Spike specific instructions to serve the cocktails personally so that he could administer the love potion to Oro's drink whilst she distracted him. She had also dressed Malveo up in a chef's outfit and ordered a host of immaculately dressed waiters and waitresses to serve the canapés from solid gold platters.

All was going well, and Madame Glittergold was already experiencing the first glow of victory. She was just beginning to imagine how she could spend Oro's fabulous wealth when somebody stood on Tootles' tail, which in turn sent the pig squealing around the room. In the ensuing chaos, the wrong drink was served to Oro, unbeknownst to Dorian Glittergold. Oro's drink ended up being served to Malveo, who drank it by accident and immediately fell in love with Tootles. Well you can imagine how bizarre everybody found Malveo's behaviour after this incident, as he professed his undying adoration to the pig and even tried to kiss the animal's snout. Naturally his mother was most perplexed, believing that Oro had taken the potion. She hurriedly shooed him back to the kitchen. "I don't know what has got into you! Now stay in there until the evening is finished," she hissed.

"My dear Dorian," said Oro suddenly appearing at her side. "Is there a problem?"

"Oh no… We're a close family that's all," she said to Oro looking distinctly embarrassed. "Malveo sees Tootles as more of a brother than a family pet….though I must admit, he is not normally given to such public displays of affection. Anyway, he has returned to the kitchen…to put the final touches to this evening's banquet."

"I don't think there is anything wrong with public displays of affection my dear lady. Shall I get you another drink?" he said deliberately allowing his hand to brush against hers as he took her glass and handed it to a waiter. "I must say, Dorian," he continued staring deeply into her eyes, "I have heard the most incredible stories of your son's talent. I am greatly looking forward to tasting some of his delicacies for myself…"

"Oh you won't be disappointed…I can assure you of that. My son is a genius and I'm not just saying that because I am his mother, though they do say the way to a man's heart is through his stomach don't they?" she simpered, sipping her newly refreshed cocktail.

"Yes they do but there are many other qualities that entice a man to fall in love."

"Of course. I suppose a man of your standing must have women throwing themselves at you?" said Dorian coyly.

Oro stroked his beard, a pained expression crossing his face. "Since my wife passed away…I have found it difficult to come to terms with my grief but I'm sure you understand - being a widow yourself. It seems we have much in common."

"Yes, it would seem we do," replied Dorian breathlessly. "Your charming daughter must miss having a mother figure in her life."

"Sadly yes. My dear sister Glace tries her best but…" he paused dramatically, "it is not the same. Anyway enough talk of the past, I always think it is better to enjoy the present…and I find the present company most agreeable. It is so refreshing to meet a lady who understands truly what it's like to shoulder the responsibility of bringing up a child…alone…in this world. You must be very proud of your son's achievements? What is his secret?"

Madame Glittergold suddenly looked rather alarmed. "Secret? There is no secret, Malveo is just extremely talented…Ah! That sounds like the dinner gong, I hope you are hungry."

Oro took her arm and whispered, "Ravenous my dear lady, absolutely ravenous."

The sight that greeted Oro Cazador as he accompanied Dorian Glittergold to the table was indeed wondrous – a full orchestra of instruments were hovering in the air, playing by themselves. Fireworks sprayed the ceiling with vibrant colours and when you walked across the floor it was as if you were dancing on the edge of the world. Statues were carved from pistachio ice cream and peach sorbet, whilst curtains woven from candyfloss hung from the windows.

"My dear lady," he said kissing her hand, "I am astounded by your generous hospitality. I have travelled Zartarbia far and wide, and never have I seen such finesse, such attention to detail."

"Oh really," Dorian tittered. "Mr Cazador…from such a great man as yourself, these compliments are undeserving I'm sure…I am, after all, just a humble hotel owner who is privileged to have such an honoured guest as yourself."

"Now, now…I have already said you must call me Oro and you must not be modest, this is indeed a most elaborate banquet that you have arranged – it quite surpasses anything I have encountered…with the exception, of course, of your beauty Dorian," he said looking deeply into her eyes.

"Mr Cazador…Oro…you're making me blush!"

"Shall we be seated?" he said. "I must say, you really look most magnificent this evening."

She giggled and said in a girly voice, "Well one likes to make an effort when one has the pleasure of such distinguished company."

"I can assure you the pleasure is all mine."

The food was more than delicious - it intoxicated each person with a feeling of euphoria that had everybody crying with laughter and feeling they had never been happier. Even Lily Rose felt a warmth that she had never felt before and, for the time being, all her problems were forgotten. By the end of the evening the normally icy Glace was dancing with Betrug and nobody wanted the night to end. Dorian was so delighted that when she went to the kitchen to fetch her son, she even allowed Isaac to eat the left over food from the dirty plates.

As she led Malveo back to the Great Hall to receive a standing ovation from the guests gathered there, she squeezed his flabby hand.

"If I am not mistaken my darling snogglepops, you have endeared yourself to Mr Cazador. He was clearly most impressed by the banquet and I believe he will propose to me before the night is done. We shall be richer than our wildest dreams. Just imagine pumpkin, we'll never have to work again!"

And she was quite right. Oro Cazador proposed to her before the various suns had risen on a new morning.

Opal Luvie smiled at her husband as they watched the couple toast their engagement. "So he has agreed the transaction then, I presume?"

"Of course! Did you have any doubt he wouldn't?"

"No, my love. You are far too clever to leave anything to chance. So when shall we have the Box of Reversals?" she asked leaning her head on his shoulder.

"Tomorrow and that is when I shall take the real chef, the secret chef – we will be long gone before our dear colleague, Mr Cazador, realises that he has been duped by that vile woman."

"Poetic justice my love, they are so well suited. I'm sure they will be very unhappy together," she murmured in his ear.

He turned to her and kissed her on the lips. "I think we can safely say that Cazador will soon be adding another skeleton to that dungeon of his."

Chapter Seventeen
BETRUG ESPION

The following morning, as the effects of the previous evening's food began to fade, all the guests were left with a weary feeling of longing and wanting more.

Lily woke up late, her hair tousled from sleep and dreams. Sunlight was streaming in through the windows and a tiny bird was perched on the end of the bed watching her.

"It's you again. Have you another message for me?" she asked gently.

The bird hopped onto the bedcovers, dropping a single red rose and an envelope towards her. She tore it open, her heart racing, and unfolded the letter.

'My dear Lily Rose,

I was really pleased to receive your letter. I keep it in my pocket so that I can read it over and over again.

I'm sorry you don't think your father would permit me to meet with you, though I understand you are the daughter of one of the most powerful men in Zartarbia and I am a just a humble gardener... but I can't stop thinking about you. The image of your beautiful face haunts me when I sleep and is the first thing I see when I awake.

Is there really no way that we could meet in secret? That is, if you want to. The garden is so lovely at this time of the year and there is much I long to show you – in the meantime I am sending a rose as a token of my admiration for you. I await your reply - Orlando'

Lily smiled to herself and picked up the bloom to smell it, allowing the delicious scent to engulf her. All she could think about was how much she longed to meet Orlando, to see his smile close up and to gaze at his handsome face. Quickly she scribbled her reply and gave it to the bird.

She stroked its soft feathers. "How I wish I could be like you. Free to come and go as I pleased, then I could meet with Orlando. Here take this to him," she said kissing the bird's head. The bird nuzzled against her neck for a moment before flying out of the window.

She lay back on the bed, clutching the precious letter. "I think I am in love," she whispered to herself.

Meanwhile…

"The FADF infiltrators are becoming far too clever for their own good," said Oro spreading out the unfolded hologram. "They are a thorn in my side."

"At least we have captured one of them and I was able to locate the rest of the bugging devices," replied Betrug, "but their equipment is becoming more sophisticated, it's true."

"So where is the girl now?" said Oro, drumming his fingers irritably.

"Agent Chloe has been transported to Segregaria. She is being held in the dungeons. What do you want me to do about the other one, this Lujzka?"

"We wait. We need to ascertain what she knows. It sounds as if there is at least one other agent in the hotel aside from her."

"I agree. It was the way she said 'that we all discussed' rather than 'we discussed'. However, until we can break the code in the hologram, we will not know for certain."

"We need to ascertain if they have other information. Does she seem particularly close to anybody else? Who have you seen her talking to?" he asked rubbing his bald head.

"There is a housekeeper Caoimhe – she is a similar age to the spy and fits the profile of a possible FADF agent. They have been working closely together. She has also spoken with the manager Pennypinch, who I have my suspicions about."

"Why?"

"My intuition says Pennypinch is a likely candidate. As you know the FADF often plant 'sleeping cells' within Syndicate territories, especially weaker ones such as Sumptitious where security is woefully inadequate. Fortuno comes here on a regular basis so possibly whoever this other spy is, has been placed here for a while to report on his activities."

"Point taken, but equally it could be somebody that has been here for a relatively short period of time."

"There was another girl who arrived at the hotel at the same time according to staff records but she is just a child, so I doubt she is working for the Federation Against Dark Forces," said the Transcender quietly.

"Keep her under surveillance all the same," instructed Oro dismissively.

"So shall I start with Pennypinch?"

"Yes, I don't trust him either, and on your way out ask Glace to set up a meeting with Fortuno."

There was a knock at the door. "Dearly beloved," said Dorian Glittergold in a sing song voice. "May I come in? I have brought some breakfast for you. Are you awake?"

Oro rolled his eyes, scowling, and signalled for Betrug to make himself scarce.

"One moment my dear," he replied in his most endearing voice, hastily going to the mirror to put on a wig. "Right I am ready now."

Madame Glittergold waddled in, followed by two waiters carrying silver trays.

"I thought after last night's excitement that you might want to enjoy a leisurely breakfast in your room," she tittered.

"How thoughtful of you, dear lady! As it happens, I am rather peckish!"

"Well don't just stand there like idiots. Lay the food out!" she snapped at the waiters and then she turned back to Oro saying sweetly, "Well tuck in my dearest, we can't have you wasting away!"

Oro sat down and had soon eaten his way through 14 rashers of bacon, 8 sausages, 12 fried eggs, 9 hash browns, 5 tins of baked beans, 16 grilled tomatoes, several loaves of bread and 20 croissants with jam and butter.

"It's so lovely to meet a man who really enjoys his food," said Dorian. "Now, I have the most wonderful surprise for you!"

"Oh yes, and what might that be?" said Oro wiping his mouth and pushing his dirty plate away.

"I have arranged a masked ball tonight in honour of our engagement and the crème de la crème of Sumptitious society will be attending! Isn't that fantastic? It will be the grandest party this land has ever seen!" announced Dorian, clutching her hands together in excitement.

"You've done what?!!!" he suddenly bellowed, pushing his chair back and slamming his hands on the table.

"My dearest beloved, I thought you would be pleased…" stammered his fiancée, shocked by his sudden anger.

"What were you thinking of!"

"I just wanted to celebrate this happy occasion," said Dorian, her face crumpling into tears as she dabbed a hanky to her eyes, "but if you don't feel the same way then…"

Cazador forced himself to calm down (though he was seething inside at the woman's stupidity).

"Now, now my dear, I'm sorry. I didn't mean to upset you…of course I am pleased, it's just that security will be difficult and once it is known that you are to be my wife…well I need to protect you and besides, I want to spend time alone with you, dearest…"

He tipped her flabby chin up to look at him. "My sweetest Dorian, please forgive my outburst. I'm a private person, a powerful man. My enemies would do anything to get to me, even if it was through you. Look I didn't mean to shout at you. I don't want us to argue…"

"Oh you silly darling!" she sniffed. "We have the rest of our lives together. Besides, it will only be two hundred of my closest friends and they are dying to meet you…oh please my beloved, it would mean so much to me!"

"Well, when you put it like that…I suppose so, but only if everybody submits themselves for a thorough security scan. And I have one other condition my sweetness…"

"What's that, my dear?" she said gazing up at him.

"Tomorrow I want us to return to Segregaria. I want us to be married straight away. Someone of your beauty and grace should not have to work… indeed, as my wife, I want to make sure you are pampered and kept in a manner befitting your new status, which is why I too have a small surprise for you," said Oro, taking something out from inside his jacket.

"What is it?"

Cazador handed her a small jewellery box. "Everything happened so fast last night and I didn't have a chance to present you with this my dearest."

"Oh, I can hardly contain myself with the excitement," she said as she opened the lid. A huge diamond ring nestled within the box. "I'm speechless!" she said, her eyes gleaming at the enormous gem.

"Here, allow me," he said taking it out and gently pushed it onto her podgy finger.

"It belonged to my mother and I have never met anybody special enough to bestow it upon.... until now."

"I don't know what to say," said Dorian.

"Say that you shall come back with me tomorrow to Segregaria."

"I would love to!" she gushed and then paused suddenly. "But I can't...what about Mr Fortuno? I cannot leave Sumptitious without his permission, he owns this land after all and it is the law here."

"I wouldn't worry about him my dear, Sumptitious will soon belong to me. You don't think that after meeting the love of my life...that I would let you slip through my fingers..."

"And what shall become of the Hotel Gastronomic?"

"You will simply close the hotel down."

"Oh my! You have thought of everything!" she trilled, admiring the ring.

"But of course dear Dorian, we shall be one big happy family. I shall be like a father to your talented son Malveo , in fact I have decided that he shall prepare the wedding feast."

The colour drained from Madame Glittergold's face. "What did you say? You want him to prepare the wedding banquet?"

"But of course...such a gifted young man! Oh don't worry, my staff will assist him in creating his culinary delights."

"No! I mean that won't be necessary, he is most particular about his recipes. He won't want anybody entering the kitchen - ever - as he always works alone. That is most important, my beloved," said Madame Glittergold, trying to cover her obvious alarm. "And you are sure you want Malveo to cook the wedding feast?"

"Is there a problem? I would have thought you would have been delighted."

"Of course there is no problem, it will be an honour for him," replied Dorian hastily.

"So be it then," he said taking her gently by the elbow and escorting her to the door. "Now as much as it pains me to be parted from you for even a moment, I have a pressing business matter that regrettably I must attend to…but I shall be eagerly counting the minutes until we are together again."

"Well, my beloved, I shall have to tear myself away from you and go to oversee tonight's festivities." She went to kiss him on the lips but as she advanced on him, he snatched her hand quickly, kissing that instead. "I am missing you already my dear."

"They say absence makes the heart grow fonder. Well, until this evening!"

He closed the door on her and went back into his room.

Glace stepped out from the shadows. "How touching love is," she said waspishly.

"Shut up! I'm simply doing what is necessary to protect my investment."

"How many times have you used that ring now?"

"How many dead wives do I have?" he said callously.

"Well she will be joining them soon enough," said Glace coldly. "In fact the sooner the better. So we leave tomorrow?"

"Yes. Is the meeting set up?"

"Devin will be here shortly," she replied as she lit a cigarette.

"I wish you wouldn't do that! It deadens my appetite and besides it's bad for your health!" he barked angrily, sitting himself down in a vast leather chair.

"Brother dear, don't be such a hypocrite – just look at yourself. If anybody needs to look after their health, it's you," she said, flicking ash onto the floor.

"Don't anger me, Glace! You're really beginning to enrage me with your constant insolence! "

"Oh shut up! I'm not one of your skivvies. Besides you've enough rage in you to fuel an army. It sweats from your pores like a repellent body odour!" she said contemptuously. "You don't frighten me brother, nor will you ever, so keep your mind focussed on the matter in hand and your mouth shut!"

"Why you vile hag! I should have you shot..." he blustered. "If it wasn't for the fact that..."

"I was your sister? Believe me brother dearest, the feeling is mutual but we are dependant on each other for the time being, so I suggest we get down to business as it is clear neither of us want to spend a moment longer than is absolutely necessary in the other's company. Now once the deal with that fool Fortuno is complete, all we need is an excuse to get the rest of The Syndicate to Segregaria. I was thinking that the joyous occasion of your forthcoming marriage would provide the perfect excuse. We use the power of the food to control them and then...then they will be putty in our hands!"

"Possibly. I agree it has to be soon but I don't want them to suspect anything until it is too late," Oro said leaning back in his chair to contemplate the best way to manipulate The Syndicate members.

The office of The Hotel Gastronomic was always a rather untidy affair with papers strewn everywhere. Spike Pennypinch was busy trying to get into the safe, where he knew all of Dorian Glittergold's secrets were kept. He had never trusted his boss but now she was to marry Cazador, he knew his time was running out. (I am sure what is quite clear to you by now was that Spike was not the most honest or pleasant of people, and he was now looking for something with which to blackmail Dorian, if it came to that. His reasoning was that he had put in all the hard work and built the hotel up to what it was, and he was damned if he was going to lose out.)

"What are you looking for?"

Spike hastily turned, startled by Dorian's voice.

"I didn't hear you come in," he said guiltily, spinning around.

"Clearly or you wouldn't be rummaging through my personal effects," she hissed.

"It's not what it looks like," said Spike, regaining his composure. "I was simply putting your affairs in order, so that everything was organised for you before your marriage to Mr Cazador."

She eyed him suspiciously. "I don't believe you. You're always sneaking around – up to something."

"I am deeply hurt by that. All I have done is serve you and the hotel!"

"Well, you won't need to for much longer. Tomorrow I leave for Segregaria," Dorian said placing her purse on a table.

"I see. So should I start to pack my things? Or would you prefer that I stay here and continue running things? After all the Hotel Gastronomic would fall to pieces without me. I can make sure everything runs smoothly in your absence," said Spike carefully.

"There's no need. Your services are no longer required. I shall be closing the hotel, and I certainly will not be needing a manager when I am Mrs Cazador!"

"So I'm just out on my ear?" Spike flared with anger. "Don't think I shall let you get away with this!"

"Sticks and stones, Mr Pennypinch, may break my bones but words will never hurt me!" she smiled.

"What about when Cazador discovers the truth? Words will break you then!"

"What do you mean?" she said, narrowing her piggy eyes.

"Oh don't you think you're a little long in the tooth to try to play the innocent! You know exactly what I am talking about!" replied Spike nastily.

Suddenly Dorian Glittergold's entire persona melted into that of Betrug Espion.

"No I don't but I am sure you will tell me!"

Chapter Eighteen
BUSINESS IS CONCLUDED

"Listen. I think something is very wrong!" said Lujzka urgently, taking Isabella to one side. "Quick! Come in here with me, we can't risk anybody seeing us!"

"How do you mean?" asked Isabella as they huddled into a darkened corner.

"I was meant to meet with Agent Chloe earlier and she didn't show up. I've been trying to find her but nobody has seen her. It is as if she has vanished into thin air."

"Do you think they are onto us?" said Isabella looking concerned.

Lujzka shook her head, "I don't know but I think the other bugging devices have been found. I haven't been able to pick up anything from Cazador's room and the ones I gave to Chloe to plant in Fortuno's private quarters are not responding either."

"What should we do?"

"We need to get into the kitchen tonight! We have to find out what they are hiding in there. I'm sure it's the key to whatever is going on."

"Do you think something has happened to Chloe?" said Isabella watching her friend's face and for the first time feeling scared.

"I don't know, but I have a feeling that we are in grave danger. There is a masked ball planned for this evening and after it is over, we go in. Then I want you to get word to the FADF. I have a terrible feeling that the hologram I gave to Chloe has been intercepted."

"I hope she's alright…"

"So do I," said Lujzka grimly. "But if she has been captured…well I dread to think…Betrug Espion is a ruthless man…"

"You think he will hurt Chloe if he has got her?" asked Isabella in a small, frightened voice.

Lujzka nodded slowly, looking terribly worried. "It is an eventuality that we have to consider."

"How awful, why would anybody want to do that?"

"There are people who are born evil. Transcenders - like Espion – well they have no feelings, no compassion…" replied Lujzka. "It has become too dangerous. You will have to leave."

"But what will you do? I don't want to leave you!" said Isabella, clutching her friend's sleeve.

"Don't worry about me," Lujzka said gently. "I can take care of myself. As soon as we have discovered what is in the kitchen, I will get you out of here. You must then get word to Detective Valise – he'll know what to do."

"How are we going to get past the security system?"

"I'll take care of that. I'm more concerned about how we unlock the kitchen door," said Lujzka, looking perplexed.

"Wait a minute! Jangle, he can do it!" exclaimed Isabella, fumbling in her pockets.

"Jangle?" said Lujzka, looking bemused.

"Yes, the key! Don't you remember? Jangle, the key…he helped me return to Zartarbia!"

"I'd forgotten about him."

"Hang on a minute…yes here he is!" she said holding the key in the air.

"And about time too!" said Jangle grumpily. "Well that's just charming! Stuff me in your pocket and forget about me!" The key folded its arms and looked around sulkily. "Anyway what's going on here?"

"We need your help Jangle," said Isabella. "We need to get into the hotel kitchen."

"I see, so that's the basis of our relationship now…you only want to be friends when YOU need something!" said the key, screwing up his metal nose in disgust.

"No, it's not like that!"

"Oh for heaven's sake, that's all we need…a stroppy key!" said Lujzka crossly.

"Who are you calling stroppy?!! I'm just highly strung that's all!"

"Don't be so ridiculous! You're a lump of metal with an attitude problem!"

"Well! I've never heard such blatant prejudice!"

"Jangle please! We need your help!" Isabella begged.

"Talk to the hand because the face ain't listening, girlfriend!" said the key petulantly.

"Oh, now you are really getting on my nerves. He's as bad as that talking compass we had to put up with when we went to visit The Thinker, do you remember?"

"Well yes, but it's true I haven't paid him any attention. Look I'm sorry Jangle, it's just that so much has been happening and we really need your help…please for me…"

"Well, maybe…but I'm doing this for you," he said to Isabella.

Lujzka rolled her eyes but refrained from saying anything.

"Well I suppose we won't know if we don't try," she concurred.

"I'll meet you back here after the masked ball is over."

"OK, I'll see you later," agreed Isabella, putting Jangle back in her pocket for safe-keeping.

Meanwhile...

"So Oro," said Devin Fortuno raising a glass of champagne, "I think that concludes our business."

"It would appear so but I will not be hurried," replied Oro.

"You have your proof," said Opal. "What more do you want?"

"I want to know why you want the Box of Reversals...what use is it to you?"

"I've told you before, it's a valuable object and my wife likes to spend money. You said yourself it is completely useless! Without the other sacred objects, it is nothing more than a valuable trinket and besides they are more myth than actuality..." drawled Devin lazily.

Oro strummed his stubby fingers on the table, watching him suspiciously. A pen and document lay between the two men.

"My dear friend, as much as I enjoy your company, I really must press you for your signature. The deal is laid out and I thought we were in agreement. You have what you set out to get. I have signed. That now makes it your turn."

"Alright I am convinced but if I find you have double-crossed me in any way..." said Oro, picking up the pen and signing.

"My friend, I simply want an easy life. Please let's leave any hostility behind us."

"There you go," said Oro gruffly handing him an object wrapped in soft cloth.

"Ah, The Box of Reversals," said Devin, unwrapping the fabric. "Well, it has been a delight doing business with you and now I shall leave you to prepare for tonight's festivities."

After Devin had gone, Oro was left feeling uneasy. Instinctively he knew he had somehow walked into a trap… but what? How? He was normally so good at knowing where problems lay. To allay his nagging doubts, he went to see his beautiful daughter whose current good mood could easily lift his own spirits.

"Lily, I have a gift for you," he said, "I want you to wear it tonight for the ball."

He held up a beautiful dress. The bodice was made from what appeared to be snow flakes that shimmered in the light. The skirt was an ornate birdcage filled with doves.

"It's lovely Papa, thank you!"

"I am so glad you like it, my dear. It's good to see you so happy. By the way, we shall be returning home tomorrow."

"Tomorrow? So soon?" said Lily, looking horrified.

"Yes, my dear. Lauren, you are to start packing immediately. We will leave first thing!"

"Can't we stay a little longer! Please Papa, it's the first time I have been outside of Segregaria and I'm really enjoying it here," she pleaded.

"No. We must go tomorrow. It's all been arranged."

He kissed his daughter's forehead. "Now then, I shall see you later and don't forget to wear the dress."

After her father had left, Lily turned and looked longingly out of the window. "I don't want to go. I will never get to meet Orlando."

"You know what your father is like, once his mind is made up."

"There must be a way," she said touching the dress as a thought came to her.

"Maybe there is…"

"What are you thinking?"

"The masked ball, don't you see? Everybody's faces will be covered."

"So?"

"We are exactly the same height and size."

"We've discussed this before, it's far too risky!"

"Yes, if we had tried to do it in Segregaria where we are constantly being watched, I agree it was too dangerous, but here the security is so much more relaxed…and besides, there will be hundreds of strangers milling around," said Lily clutching Lauren's hand urgently. "Please…I couldn't bear to leave without meeting him at least once!"

"Your father will know I'm not you – he'll kill me," Lauren shrank back from Lily's hand.

"No he won't. You just have to speak as little as possible and when you do then you imitate my voice. We will both wear wigs and heavy make-up round our eyes. I promise he won't guess."

"You know I would do anything for you but…I'm sorry I can't," Lauren said nervously.

"My father thinks I am content because I am with him. He thinks he has his little girl back again, I see it in his eyes, he suspects nothing. All you have to do is wear the dress and mask that he bought for me and I shall wear yours, then during the course of the evening I will slip away to meet Orlando," said Lily.

"Is he really worth it?" Lauren asked. She had always desperately pitied Lily who, for all her wealth and beauty, had to be one of the most unhappy girls she had ever met.

"Oh yes! I know you're frightened, but there's no need. Nothing will go wrong," she said squeezing Lauren's hand reassuringly. Lauren looked into Lily's shining eyes and knew she had to help her friend.

"Alright then I'll do it."

Chapter Nineteen
THE MASKED BALL

The clock struck 7pm, a loud hollow sound that reverberated around the hotel. Lady Dee and Lady Dah were seated in the salon, already dressed in their costumes for the ball. Lady Dee wore a gown made from peacock feathers with a bejewelled mask to match and her twin wore a dress covered with ostrich plumes.

"Well she should be here any moment. You need to speak to her before all the other guests arrive," said Lady Dah to her sister.

Lady Dee looked aggrieved. "Why can't you speak to her?"

"You drew the short straw…it was agreed. If they marry, then where will that leave us?" whispered Lady Dah.

"SShhh! She's coming," said Lady Dee, nudging her twin.

"Dearest cousin how perfectly divine you look!" said Lady Dah.

"Yes, absolutely heavenly. Mr Cazador won't be able to take his eyes off you!" agreed her twin, putting her fan over her mouth to conceal her mirth, for Dorian Glittergold looked utterly hideous. She was dressed in a frothy pink outfit that gave her the appearance of a giant meringue. Her mask was the only redeeming part of the outfit because it covered her face.

"So cousin dear, Mr Cazador seems most…" said Lady Dee.

"…charming," finished Lady Dah.

"Clearly he has fantastic…" purred her sister. "

"…taste," interjected Lady Dee. "He's obviously most enamoured with you, cousin dearest. How exciting that he proposed to you straight away. How lucky you are!"

"And the ring he has given you is…"

"…stunning! Quite stunning!"

"…and expensive, that must be worth a small fortune!"

"It is beautiful, isn't it?" simpered the revolting Dorian Glittergold, patting her coiled hair.

"Oh yes!" said the sisters in unison.

"I'm so nervous…do I look alright? Do you think this outfit makes me look fat?" said Dorian smoothing her hands over her huge hips.

"Oh no…You look quite divine," soothed Lady Dah.

"There's no need for concern," added Lady Dee, who was thoroughly enjoying the duplicity. "How could he resist you? After all you are to be married."

"But do you think he really loves me?"

"Yes, cousin dear, as much as you love him. Nothing can go wrong, rest assured," said Lady Dee.

The two sisters looked at each other, knowing that all they were interested in was finding out what would become of them. Dorian had been their meal ticket all their lives, after all.

"Cousin dearest, why don't I get you a glass of champagne to steady your nerves? Sister darling, you stay and keep Dorian company," said Lady Dah, shooting a look at her twin that clearly meant 'well ask her then!' and, with that, she left them to it.

"Oh, wait a moment. You have a little lipstick on your teeth," said Lady Dee producing a hankie. "Here let me wipe it off for you."

Dorian opened her huge mouth and the other woman wiped off the make up feeling rather sick at the sight of her cousin's large yellow buck teeth.

"There. All done, my dear. So, do you think you will be happy living in Segregaria?" Lady Dee asked.

Dorian tittered. "We have only just met, but I am confident that I shall make the perfect wife for him – besides who can be unhappy when faced with a life of luxury?"

"Well, whatever your plan was, it obviously worked. I am delighted for you," said Lady Dee with false brightness.

"I know he's not much to look at but he has other assets like…his manners. It's always nice to meet a gentleman who will look after one."

"Absolutely. A lady such as yourself should be treated properly…and of course he is rich beyond your wildest dreams…" crooned Lady Dee.

Madame Glittergold looked at her cousin sharply. "I hope you're not implying my interest in Mr Cazador is purely monetary! Though I must say such generosity in a man is certainly not unwelcome!"

"I couldn't agree more, cousin dear!" exclaimed Lady Dee. "Your destiny has always been for grander things, the finer things in life and at last it looks as if that is finally coming true."

Dorian smiled, "This is true."

Lady Dee cleared her throat delicately. "When you are married, my dear cousin… you will be living like a queen and rightly so, but…you won't forget about us, will you? I mean, after all, we are your most loyal and trusted companions."

"So it's not my welfare you're interested in, but your own," snapped Dorian narrowing her eyes. "I might have known."

"No! No, what a terrible thing to say, we only want what is best

Oro Cazadort
his sister Glace
at
The Masked Ball

for you….t's just that it would break our hearts to be parted from you, from Malveo and darling Tootles. We are family after all!" said Lady Dee attempting to look hurt, "You are all we have in this world!"

"I'm sorry, cousin…please don't distress yourself. Of course you shall be coming to live with us," soothed Dorian, because she had come to rely on her cousins' constant flattery. "Now, now compose yourself - our guests will be here any moment."

"Yes, you are right of course cousin dear, we must focus on the matter in hand – your future happiness!" said Lady Dee, relieved to know that their future was safe. She smiled conspiratorially at Lady Dah who was watching her like a hawk from across the room.

Hundreds of guests arrived over the following hour to offer their congratulations to Madame Glittergold and Oro Cazador. All of them were wearing the most magnificent costumes and the hotel sparkled with colour. Tiny fairies circled overhead holding lanterns that changed colour as they moved from room to room. Magic dust swirled and shimmered in the air. Betrug stood in the shadows, keeping a watchful eye on everybody. Lily and Lauren were almost the last to arrive, having made the switch. Both their faces were totally obscured with elaborate masks.

"We'll circulate for a few moments, and then I'll slip out into the garden," whispered Lily, disguised as Lauren.

Lily's heart was pounding with excitement as she quietly made her way out of the door, down the long corridor that led to the leafy expanse of the garden. The night sky was saturated with stars and moons as she made her way to the appointed meeting place.

"Orlando? Orlando? Are you there?" she whispered into the gloom.

"Lily is that you?"

"Yes, where are you?"

Orlando stepped out from the shadows. "Quick. Follow me, before anybody sees us!"

He took her hand, leading her away from the hotel. They walked until they reached a pavilion covered with ivy and flowers that overlooked a lake. The water was like a mirror except for a couple of swans that glided towards them.

"I can't believe we've been able to meet."

"Nor me. I can't stay too long though – Lauren is taking a massive risk."

"So what do you think?" he said gesturing to the expansive garden.

"It's so beautiful here," said Lily gazing across the lake.

"Do you know that when swans mate, they mate for life," he said gazing at the birds swimming in the moonlight.

"That's how true love should be," she replied.

"Can I ask you something?" said Orlando, gently turning her to face him. "Do you believe in love at first sight?"

"I think so, I mean, I've never been in love..,"

"Me neither, but what I feel for you is driving me crazy."

"I know and I feel the same way."

"You do?"

Lily nodded. "Yes, but there is no hope for us. My father would never allow us to be together."

"What are we going to do?" sighed Orlando.

She shook her head. "I don't know...Listen I have something to tell you, my father is insisting that we return home tomorrow. I don't want to go but I have no choice."

"Tomorrow? But that's so soon!"

"Maybe we can continue to write to each other? It will be difficult because of the security in Segregaria but…"

"I don't want to lose you Lily," he said urgently.

"You won't. You will be in my thoughts and heart," she whispered, kissing him lightly on the lips. "I must go now before my father realises what I have done."

"I will find a way to reach you," he promised, reluctant to let her go.

"Goodbye Orlando," she said, slipping off into the darkness.

Opal Luvie was putting the finishing touches to her outfit, watching her husband's reflection in the mirror. "Are you ready? We shall be late for the ball."

She stood up and opened to the door of their suite, trying to hurry her husband up. Devin was staring into his crystal ball, looking preoccupied.

"What are you doing my darling?" she asked. His hands glided over the smooth surface of the ball in a series of complex patterns.

"Can't you do that later my love?" she urged, keen to get downstairs and observe their plan unfolding.

"I don't believe it!" exclaimed Devin Fortuno, looking up at her. "She's here - see for yourself!"

Opal Luvie hurried over to where he sat, and leaning over, she strained to see inside the crystal ball. "Who? I can't see anything."

"The human child, the one with the Locket of Fire and Water, she's here…in the hotel!" Devin's voice was incredulous.

"How can that be possible? How could you have not seen it before?" asked Opal, studying the pale image of Isabella's face within the ball.

"I don't know…the magic of the locket must have strengthened since she was last here, it must be protecting her."

"Where exactly is she? I can't make it out!"

"I don't know…no wait she's downstairs in The Great Hall."

"Well what are we waiting for! Let's go and search for her!" said Opal her dark eyes gleaming.

"We must have that locket even if I have to cut off the girl's head to get it!" said Devin putting on a flowing cloak and a mask made from black raven's feathers. He held his arm out to his wife. "Shall we, my dear?"

"Oh yes, she won't escape us this time!" They swept out of their suite and down the long corridor, unaware that Lujzka had overheard their conversation.

Lujzka ran as silently as possible down the back staircase to where she knew Isabella was.

"We have to enter the kitchen now," she said breathlessly.

"I thought we were going to wait until the ball had finished," replied Isabella.

"There's no time! Devin knows you are here and he's coming to find you. We have to go straight away. Come on!" said Lujzka grabbing her hand.

"What about the alarm system?"

"I've dealt with it."

"Somebody will see us!"

"They won't," she replied taking from her pocket what could only be described as a long open zip which she attached to Isabella's feet. "When I pull this up you will become invisible."

"OK, if you say so," said Isabella stifling her amazement. In the midst of all the craziness she experienced in Zartarbia, she occasionally paused to observe the more bizarre happenings. This was certainly one of them, she thought as she watched Lujzka zip her image away before doing the same to herself.

They crept towards the kitchen door, as waiters darted this way and that. Finally they came to the area where all were forbidden.

"Quick, get that key out," whispered Lujzka.

"Suppose whatever is inside is dangerous?" said Isabella taking Jangle out from her pocket.

"It's a chance we will have to take. Now come on before Devin tracks us down!"

"OK. It's up to you now Jangle…do your stuff!"

The key studied the lock, metamorphosing rapidly until he was the right shape to open the door. The lock clicked open.

"Here we go then," said Lujzka, twisting the handle.

Chapter Twenty
RESCUING THE SECRET CHEF

They quickly stepped through the doorway into a hive of activity. Pots and pans were flying around the room, carrying various delicious sauces. Whisks were beating eggs, spoons stirring custard and all were so busy that they did not hear the door close. At the centre of this commotion, the girls could just about make out a figure through the steam. As they moved closer, they could see Isaac more clearly, with his scarred body and matted fur. Abruptly he looked up, sniffing the air.

"Is somebody there?" he asked timidly, turning around.

"It's alright, we won't harm you," said Lujzka unzipping herself from the invisibility suit and helping Isabella out of hers.

"You're not allowed in here! Madame Glittergold will find…you must go now. You really must before she discovers you. She'll blame me otherwise!" said the child, his voice full of horror.

"It's alright. Please, we're here to help. I'm FADF agent Lujzka. I won't let anybody hurt you! I'm guessing that you are the real chef."

Isaac backed into a corner, his face crumpled with panic. "It's a secret! You mustn't tell or she'll kill me! You have to leave."

The magic cutlery immediately rushed over to him, forming a protective circle around the terrified child.

"Get back! You leave Isaac alone!" shouted Glinty, the knife, waving his blade at them.

"Come a step nearer and I'll batter yer," yelled Mrs Roly.

Lujzka raised her hands in a gesture of reassurance. "Please I promise, I mean no harm. We're here to help. This is Isabella. She wears the Locket of Fire and Water, and has come from her own world to Zartarbia. It was she that destroyed Sectica and her tyrannical reign of Tivany and Narcissimal."

"I've a cousin that lives in Tivany," said Mr Bristles the broom. "I heard all about that."

"Look, I believe that Isaac's life is in great danger. I think he is the reason for Oro Cazador's visit here – that he wants to use his magic powers for his own evil plans!"

The magic cutlery muttered for a moment between themselves before dropping away from around the boy.

Isabella slowly stepped towards Isaac in amazement. "It's you! You're the boy I saw in my dream."

Lujzka turned to her, "You didn't mention that before."

"With everything that was going on, I forgot."

"What do you mean 'her own world'?" asked Glinty looking puzzled. "What nonsense is this?"

"There is no time to explain, but it's not safe for either of you to stay here," said Lujzka urgently.

Isaac looked at Isabella, his huge eyes blinking. "You seem familiar to me too but I don't know why."

"Listen, me dear," Mrs Roly said gently to the boy. "The FADF are the good 'uns. This could be yer only chance ter escape the ole cow and I think you should take it."

The rest of the magic cutlery nodded.

"We'll cover for you young man, give you a head start," said Mr Bristles.

"But I don't want to leave you," said Isaac.

"Don't you worry," said Glinty. "We can look after ourselves. Mr Bristles is right, you won't stand a chance if the food stops coming out from the kitchen."

"Are we going to use the invisibility suits to get him out of here?" asked Isabella.

"No, they can only be used once. And besides, we need to get you both somewhere away from here. Is there anywhere safe for you to go to, Isaac?"

"The rats, I suppose. King Pizarro will help, I'm sure, but he lives in the sewers and we're too big to get down there," said Isaac pointing to the drain cover.

"No you're not. I'm going to shrink you both so that you can fit," she said, producing what appeared to be a calculator from her pocket.

"What's that?" asked Isaac dubiously.

"It's a standard issue miniaturiser. Don't worry it won't hurt at all. Now listen to me carefully…I want you to make your way to this rat kingdom."

The children nodded.

"Go to them. Nobody will be able to get to you there – it's the safest place for both of you at the moment. I want you to inform the FADF of what has happened. Take this Isabella," she said urgently, handing a ring to her. "It has a transmitter inside. If you run into difficulties open the top like so and press this button, it will send an emergency signal to Detective Valise. Right, we have no time to waste. We need to construct some sort of vessel for you to travel in…now what is going to be best for a boat – quick think of something that will float and is durable?"

Lujzka turned around, quickly scanning the kitchen.

"What about me?" piped up Mrs Cosy the teapot. "I would make a good boat."

"Great, yes perfect! Now Isabella, see if you can find some sort of fabric to act as a sail…what else are we going to need?"

"I could be a mast," said Prongo the fork jumping out of the cutlery drawer, closely followed by two teaspoons.

"Yeah and we can be paddles!" said Scoopy and Shiner. "Oh please, we want to come too."

Lujzka nodded. "Alright. Now we need to work quickly. Isabella what have you got there?"

"A handkerchief. Is it big enough?" she said, handing it over.

"Fine. Now I need some string or thread and something sticky like some sweets or something. Have you got anything like that Isaac?"

"There are some marshmallows over there," he replied. "I don't have any string, but there's some old cooked spaghetti in the fridge."

"Good that will do…well hurry, hurry! There's not a moment to lose."

Isabella and Isaac watched curiously as Lujzka quickly transformed the teapot into a boat. Using the fork and a pencil to make a mast she lashed them together with the spaghetti.

"Hey that tickles," giggled Prongo as she wound the pasta around him.

"Hold still will you!" snapped Lujzka as she then tied the corners of the handkerchief to the top and bottom to form a sail. Finally she cut open a marshmallow, using the sugary substance to hold the mast.

"Now it's time to shrink you both," she said. Tapping some

numbers into the miniaturiser, she then pressed the device to each of their foreheads. Isabella immediately felt an odd tingling sensation, like pins and needles as she started getting smaller and smaller. It felt as if she was being sucked into herself. In a matter of moments she and Isaac were no taller than a pair of sparrows. They scrambled into the makeshift boat and Lujzka handed them the two teaspoons and a box of matches. "These might come in handy as it's going to be really dark down there…Oh, I almost forgot…take this," she said handing them a small bottle of strange looking potion, 'It will restore you to your normal sizes in an instant. Now go, and good luck!"

"Have a safe journey! We'll be thinking of you! Goodbye! Good Luck!" chorused the rest of the Magic Cutlery.

Lujzka gently lowered them down into the drain, which was a bit of a tight squeeze because of Mrs Cosy's spout.

"Be careful not to chip me," she said nervously.

Finally Lujzka got them safely into the drain and quickly pulled the grid back over. That task complete, Lujzka thanked the remaining cutlery and crockery before quietly slipping out of the kitchen, using Jangle to lock the door behind them. She waited a moment to check nobody was around and began to make her way through the back corridors when she thought she could hear footsteps. She held her breath, heart pounding, waiting in silence. The footsteps became louder and she could just about make out the voices of Devin and Opal talking quietly. It seemed an age before they faded into the distance.

Finally, when she was certain the coast was clear, she quickly made her way through a deserted conference room. It looked rather sinister as the drawn curtains blocked out the moonlight outside. She wished she had brought a torch now, as she gingerly felt her way across the room. Lujzka had almost reached the other side when suddenly there was the sharp roll of flint, as somebody lit a cigarette. Just a few feet away from her was Betrug Espion, his face glowing eerily through the smoke. He was sitting at a grand piano.

"Oh you gave me quite a fright!" Lujzka said reverting back to her waitress guise. "I…I didn't realise that there was anybody in here. I thought everybody was at the masked ball."

He slowly got up, trailing a finger over the piano keys as he moved towards her.

"So what are you doing down here then?" he said slowly, taking a drag of his cigarette.

"I was…er…fetching some napkins for breakfast tomorrow," said Lujzka hastily.

Betrug walked over to the door, blocking her way with his arm. "That's curious, as I know this hotel quite well by now. I happen to know they are kept in the morning room, situated on the other side of the hotel."

"Madame Glittergold wanted me to fetch some special ones that she keeps in here."

"I think we both know that isn't true."

"I don't know what you mean, Sir," said Lujzka. "Anyway I have an early start tomorrow, so if you'll excuse me I need to go to bed."

Betrug didn't move. "You've been a busy little bee."

"I said I have to go," she said firmly.

He took a sharp drag of his cigarette and threw it to the floor, stubbing it out with the metal toe of his boot.

"Let me pass!. You have no reason to detain me," Lujzka said, looking him directly in the eye.

He lifted his arm abruptly. "Yes, of course. Where are my manners?" he said, gesturing for her to pass.

"Well goodnight, Sir," she said as she turned to hurry through the doorway.

"Just one last thing my dear, where are the napkins?"

"Sorry?"

"The napkins you were fetching for your mistress," said Betrug licking his lip.

"Somebody else must have already collected them," said Lujzka, turning round and smiling weakly. She turned to leave the room.

"I see, well goodnight...Agent Lujzka."

In a split second she felt a sharp blow to the back of her neck and then darkness swallowed her up.

"Sweet dreams, my dear," sneered Betrug, failing to notice the metal key that had fallen from her pocket. Jangle watched helplessly as Betrug lifted her body over his shoulder and carried her away.

Chapter Twenty-One
INSIDE THE SEWERS

The light of the kitchen quickly evaporated into dank darkness as the current of the drains took them. Dirty water sloshed and swilled loudly against the sides of the walls. The stench was quite revolting, a combination of brussel sprouts and stink bombs. Isabella was convinced she was going to vomit but Isaac seemed unaffected by it.

"I think I'm going to be sick!" she shouted as the flow and speed of the water became faster.

"There's no time for that!" he pointed his finger ahead. "It looks as if we're about to go over a waterfall!"

"A what? What did you say?" screamed Isabella, straining to hear him.

"I said hold tight, we about to go over…" and with that they found themselves crashing over the edge. The force of the waterfall was phenomenal and a moment later their make shift boat smacked into the swirling froth at the bottom. Isabella almost lost Scoopy, who was acting as her paddle.

"Don't let go!" the little teaspoon shrieked. "Hold on to me!" but as she tried to grab hold of him with both hands, the ring transmitter that Lujzka had given her slipped off her small finger and dropped into the murky water.

"The transmitter! I've lost it!" she yelled to Isaac.

"That's the least of our problems!" he shouted back. "We'll be lucky if the boat's not smashed to pieces – everybody hold tight!"

There was no time to feel afraid. They had to paddle furiously to stop the teapot from being smashed into the walls of the sewer. They were spinning in a gushing vortex of water and rubbish. It seemed like an eternity until the speed of the current gradually subsided and they were able to guide the make shift boat into what appeared to be some sort of cave. They dragged the vessel onto a dry ledge and collapsed on the floor, trying to catch their breath.

"Is everybody alright?" asked Isabella.

"Wow! What a blast! Can we do it again?" said the teaspoons excitedly as she lay them down on a pebble.

"No we can't," said Isabella aghast that anyone would want to go through that again. "Mrs Cosy? Are you hurt?"

The teapot sneezed. "No dear, just a little shaken."

"Well my nerves are shot to pieces!" exclaimed Prongo melodramatically. "And I feel one of my headaches coming on."

"Stop feeling sorry for yourself you daft fork! You've been safely sitting inside me while I've faced all the danger!" retorted the teapot tartly.

"What do you mean 'faced all the danger'? I almost came unstuck when we went over that waterfall!" snapped the fork.

"Come on you two, don't argue," said Isaac wearily. "We're all tired, cold and wet. We need to make a fire, otherwise we'll freeze to death."

Isabella picked out the box of matches and tried to light one. "It's no good. They're all wet. Have a look around, see if you can find anything with which to start a fire."

Slowly Isabella's eyes became more accustomed to the dim and dingy surroundings. Aside from the expected bags of rotting food, there was a plastic key ring with a picture of a shell on it, a ladies purse filled with coins, a pair of sewing scissors, a couple of old newspapers and a soggy teddy bear.

"I think I've found something!" called Isaac. "It looks like a lighter!"

"Great, I've got some paper."

She started to heap together some of the rubbish as Isaac dragged the lighter over. He was weak with hunger and the ordeal they had just been through. Together they managed to get a small fire started, then Isabella slumped down onto a half eaten box of popcorn whilst Isaac sat on a discarded necktie - both exhausted from their journey.

"Well I don't want to do that again... we were almost killed," said Isabella, feeling shattered. "So have you any idea where we are or how we get to this rat palace?"

"Not exactly," said Isaac. "But they have look outs that regularly patrol the sewers. I'm sure we'll come across one of them soon."

"Oh great! So what you're really saying is that we're lost, stuck here in this filthy place with no way of contacting the FADF or these rat friends of yours!"

"Don't blame me! It's that friend of yours who has got us into this mess."

"Well, how ungrateful! We rescued you!" Isabella retorted crossly.

"Rescued me! That's a laugh...!"

"Now, now, now children – we're all a little over-wrought," interrupted the teapot.

"Wait a moment, I almost forgot. Lujzka gave me a special

Isabella + Isaac
trying to reach
The Rat Kingdom

holographic telegram that will deliver itself directly to the FADF," said Isabella hastily checking her pockets. "It must be here somewhere, ah yes…look here it is!"

"Well what are we waiting for? Send it!" said Isaac.

"What shall I say?" asked Isabella.

"Just explain what has happened at the hotel and that we are heading for The Kingdom of Discarded Treasure and Water."

Quickly Isabella scribbled a message that the telegram automatically transcribed into a series of images and words, sort of like watching a video with subtitles.

When she was finished she folded it and held it out into the darkness of the sewer. The telegram began to glow like a firefly and then took off.

"Let's hope it works," she said quietly. "I don't fancy being stuck down here forever."

"Today's been quite an ordeal. I think we should all try and get some sleep," said Mrs Cosy. "You need to keep your strength up."

"What about the fire? We can't let it go out if we are to be found. We need a signal so that these patrols can see us," said Isabella sleepily.

"I'll keep an eye on it, my dear. You go to sleep."

Isabella pulled an old glove over herself and curled up, quickly succumbing to an uncomfortable sleep.

Chapter Twenty-Two
SHADOWS AND DANGER

The following morning Madame Glittergold was busy applying more mascara to her already heavily coated eyelashes (giving the appearance that she had two tarantulas stuck to her lids) when Oro Cazador stormed in, slamming the door hard.

"You startled me!" said Dorian, accidentally smudging her make up. "Whatever is the matter beloved? You look a little vexed!"

Oro stalked over to her, his hands clasped firmly behind his back.

"Vexed? You think I appear vexed?" he said sarcastically, his glass eye glaring at her. "Why would you think that?"

"All I meant is you seem a touch out of sorts. Shall I fetch you a nice cup of tea?" she replied nervously, moving to stand up.

"Sit down!" he roared, "I don't want any sodding tea! And as for being a little vexed - as you put it - I'm furious, livid! I AM ENRAGED!"

"My dearest, whatever is the matter?" said Dorian looking extremely alarmed.

"I asked one simple thing of you and you have let me down! Did I not emphasis the importance of strict security during my visit here?" he stabbed a finger at her.

"Yes of course but…"

"Shut up! When I TALK you LISTEN! Do you understand?" he roared at her, his one real eye bulging in its socket.

"You're frightening me!"

"Good, perhaps you will begin to understand the meaning of respect. Now do you understand?" he snarled, grabbing her shoulders.

"Yes, but what am I meant to have done?"

"I want you to tell me how it was possible that FADF agents have been discovered working here undercover! Spying on me!" he bellowed.

"I don't understand…please you're hurting me!" whimpered Dorian trying to back away from him.

He let go of her shoulders abruptly.

"Betrug captured not just one but two spies, both working as members of your staff, which leads me to pose the question as to how many others there might be that have foiled your security checks! This is your hotel, is it not?"

"You know it is."

He took a deep breath and rubbed his forehead. "Then I will ask you again, how could you have allowed such a blatant breach of security to occur?"

"I really couldn't say, honestly. Mr Pennypinch is responsible for hiring and firing of staff – my dearest, you must believe me!"

"I am greatly disappointed in you," he said gravely, turning his back on her. "Maybe I have been mistaken in my affections for you…"

"Please, my beloved, don't say that! Don't be angry with me. Truly, I am as perplexed as you are! I will summon Spike straight away and we will get to the bottom of this matter…" she said wringing her hands.

Oro slowly circled around her, watching her closely. "Well, that is the other interesting thing. It would seem that your precious hotel manager has absconded."

Dorian looked shocked. "He can't have!"

He rounded on her. "Well he has. Am I to conclude that I can't trust my future wife?"

"Of course you can trust me. Please my dearest, I can't bear it that you are so cross with me. I would do anything to prove my love for you, anything you ask."

"Anything?"

"Yes, just say the word my love," she said pleadingly.

"I want you to sign over custody of Malveo to me."

Dorian blinked, looking momentarily confused. "Malveo?"

"Yes, as a precaution you understand, so that I can protect him as well as you."

"Alright my love, if it will set your mind at ease."

His face suddenly softened, the anger dissolving from his expression.

"It will, my dearest," he said, handing her a pen and paper. "I'm sorry if I alarmed you but as I have said before, I have many enemies. I want us to be safe, untouchable and clearly it is not safe for us here. We must leave immediately, my dear," he said gently, as he stroked the side of her face.

"Immediately?"

"Yes, I just want what is best for us. Now finish getting ready."

Dorian nodded, smiling weakly as he kissed her brusquely on the hand.

"I'll see you downstairs in one hour."

"An hour? I'm going to need more time than that!"

"No you won't. Everything you shall need as my wife awaits you at Segregaria."

The moment Oro had left, Dorian quickly slipped out of her room and down to Spike's quarters. The bed hadn't been slept in and there were no clothes in the cupboard or drawers. She then went to the office to be confronted by total disarray – papers were scattered across the floor, furniture upturned and the safe had been forced open. At least she had removed any incriminating documents relating to her stepson before Oro's arrival. She knew she had to act quickly. Where was Spike? Why had he left?

She hastened to the kitchen, anxiously fumbling with the keys to open the door. The room was deathly quiet. She scanned the room, panic welling up inside her. "Where are you? Show yourself!"

Her voice echoed emptily.

"Get out here now you little rat or God help me I will thrash you to within an inch of your life!"

"No you won't!"

Dorian spun around, trying to ascertain where the voice had come from.

"Who's there?" she said, clearly startled. "Show yourself! Where is the monster?"

"Don't call 'im that!" shrieked Mrs Roly, butting into Dorian's large backside and knocking her over, "Yer bully!"

Dorian thudded onto the floor, landing heavily. As she rolled over she found herself face to face with the magic cutlery.

"Who the hell are you?!" she exclaimed scrambling to her feet.

"Never yer mind. I gotta a good mind to giv you a frashing, yer old hag!"

"Where's the brat?"

"I told yer not to call 'im fings like that. E's gone and 'e 'ain't comin' back."

Dorian Glittergold's heart felt as if it was sinking in quicksand.

"Yes, he's gone and you're never going to be able to hurt the lad again!" said Mr Bristles.

"Gone where?" she shrieked.

"Far away from here, where you'll never find him!" said the broom.

"No! No! this can't be happening!" Madame Glittergold gasped as she staggered out of the kitchen, locking the door behind her.

Lady Dee and Lady Dah were packing the last of their possessions when their cousin burst in, looking most distraught.

"Dorian, my dear, whatever is the matter?" asked Lady Dee.

"I… I… I think I'm going to faint. The most terrible thing has happened!" said Dorian frantically.

Lady Dah pulled out a chair. "Sit down darling cousin and tell us what has happened! Quick, sister, get the smelling salts!"

"You look quite terrible!" said Lady Dee, hastily wafting a bottle under Dorian's nose.

"They're gone!!" she wailed. "I don't know what I shall do!"

"Who?" asked Lady Dee, flashing her sister a look.

"Mr Pennypinch…his room is empty…the office has been ransacked…"

"We did try to warn you. We always said he was no good!" said Lady Dah, pursing her lips.

"I hate to say it but we told you so," added her twin, trying not to look smug.

"Never mind, you have no need of him now. You have us," comforted Lady Dah.

"It's much worse than that. I don't know what to do!" howled Madame Glittergold burying her head in her hands.

"No point crying over split milk…" began Lady Dee.

"…and besides we're here to help," said Lady Dah, stroking Dorian's hair.

"We've always here to help and offer our advice…" said Lady Dee.

"…as humble as it is," added Lady Dah pointedly.

"No you don't understand…the boy's gone as well! My chef has escaped!"

The two sisters looked at each other in surprise.

"But we saw Malveo just moments ago, with Tootles," said Lady Dee.

"No, not Malveo! The REAL chef - he's gone, escaped, don't you understand! Oro thinks Malveo is going to create our wedding banquet and well…he can't!"

"What are you saying? Malveo isn't the chef?"

"No!" sobbed Dorian.

"You've been deceiving everybody all along?" asked Lady Dee, astounded.

"You've lied to US!" said Lady Dah, getting up and pacing around.

"We're your most trusted companions – you should have told us!" wailed Lady Dee.

"So who is the real chef?"

"My stepson," admitted Dorian.

"Isaac? I thought you'd packed him off to live with distant relatives," said Lady Dee looking perplexed.

"I thought you couldn't stand him?" added her sister.

"Well, I didn't. He creates the food and without him there can be no wedding feast," she snivelled.

"EXACTLY how bad is Malveo at cooking? I mean would he be able to pull it off, so to speak?" asked Lady Dah.

"No, he can't even make beans on toast. But on top of that, two FADF agents have been apprehended by Oro's body guard and he was furious! I've never seen him like that before! I don't know what to do!"

The two sisters nodded to one another and calmly hugged Dorian.

"Alright, don't worry - the fact of the matter is that we are all in this together. If Oro Cazador finds out, we are all back to square one!"

"And we can't have that – obviously you had your reasons, cousin dear," said Lady Dah.,

"I mean, he's not marrying you for the child's cookery skills – is he?" reasoned Lady Dee.

"No! Of course he's not!" agreed Lady Dah.

"But he is insisting that Malveo creates the wedding banquet!" said Dorian, giving out an enormous wail. "He will know I have deceived him!"

"There, there. You mustn't distress yourself."

"We shall think of something," said Lady Dee.

"But all that's left is a kitchen full of magic cutlery. There's nothing for it but to call off the wedding - or at least postpone it!" said Madame Glittergold melodramatically.

The sisters looked at each other, sharing a sense of horror. The last thing they wanted was to lose the untold riches that would come with their cousin's union to Oro Cazador.

"No, you can't do that!"

"You mustn't! Did you say magic cutlery?"

"Yes, it belongs to the brat…I mean I had no idea they were magic," sniffed Dorian.

"Well there it is. A solution to the problem!" exclaimed Lady Dee. "Don't you see? It's not this brat that creates the enchanted food – it's the cutlery!"

"Yes, all we need to do is to get them to work for Malveo," nodded her sister.

"But, he'll know, he will find out that I've lied him! He'll never forgive me… and they seemed a rather hostile bunch of utensils!"

"They're simply pots and pans, for heaven's sake!" said Lady Dah.

"But what if they refuse?" said Dorian.

"You leave them to us," smiled Lady Dee slyly.

"Yes, we'll persuade them," added her twin craftily.

Outside Oro Cazador's entourage was preparing for departure. Carriages had been adorned with fresh flowers and spinning planets. Most of his guests were already settled, enjoying refreshments and listening to a floating sitar player. Footmen had been rushing around, collecting luggage, plumping up cush-ions and generally attending to whatever demand was thrown at them.

"Where is that woman?" he snarled to his sister Glace, checking his watch.

"No doubt she is busy beautifying herself for you, readying herself for your wedding night," she replied sardonically.

"Shut up!"

"Somebody's tetchy!" she smirked. "I don't understand why you have to marry the woman now anyway. You have ownership of the boy."

"Appearances must be maintained. I can't afford to arouse the suspicions of The Syndicate or the FADF until I have them where I want them."

At that precise moment, Madame Glittergold and her cousins appeared in the doorway, followed by a trail of bellboys struggling to carry loads of heavy suitcases. Mr Moulder led them, staggering along with some hat boxes.

"My dear, I was beginning to get worried and you've kept everybody waiting," said Cazador gripping her elbow and hurriedly escorting her to an awaiting carriage.

"We really must depart straight away."

"Yes, my love, I just had a few things to pack."

"Why do you need all of this? I told you that everything you could ever need would be waiting for you at Segregaria! What's in these anyway? And why are they making a clanking sound? It looks as if you've packed everything except the kitchen sink!" Oro said, not knowing how right he was.

"It was a few things that Malveo needed. You see, he can only work with his own equipment, my dearest," said Madame Glittergold.

"Well if you feel it is essential to his performance, I suppose a genius must work with his own tools. I have arranged that you shall travel with your cousins in this carriage and Malveo will travel with me. It will give us a chance to get to know each other better. I have great plans for him."

"He's used to being with myself and Tootles…"

"No! We need time to bond - father to son, so to speak. I am eager to know the secrets of his fabulous food," said Oro, brushing a strand of hair from her face. "We have much to discuss as I am sure he will be a great asset to my business."

"He is very coy, my love. In fact he is most protective of his work," she said with concern. "Really quite temperamental. You know what these creative types can be like…perhaps it would be best to wait until we have arrived at our new home, got settled in…"

"Dorian my dearest, it is my wish. Now please send him to me straight away. When we are married my dear, I don't want you contradicting me. If I ask you to do something then I expect you to do it without hesitation."

"I shall send him to you immediately, my love," she said anxiously, hesitating for a split second.

"Good girl," he replied. "By the way I have a little gift for you by way of an apology for my earlier outburst."

"Really?"

"This is for you, my beloved," he said, producing a stunning necklace. "Believe me when I say that I want nothing more than the happiness of my family."

"Oh, Oro! I don't know what to say…"

(Let me remind you she was a woman who was easily won over, so any worries about his appalling behaviour were immediately forgotten).

"Good, my darling. I shall see you when we arrive at Segregaria," he said, blowing her a kiss.

And with that he marched along the length of his entourage, passing his daughter, Lauren and Betrug as he went. Lily followed his progress from inside her carriage, feeling utterly miserable. All she could think about was Orlando and the fact she would never see him again. Lily wished she and Lauren were alone so that they could talk freely, but her father's bodyguard was under orders not to let them out of his sight until they had reached the safety of Segregaria.

They were just about to set off and the footmen were securing the doors of all the travel compartments. She gazed up to the sky, wondering if this would be the last time she would be able to feel the sun on her face or whether she was doomed to spend the rest of her life under her father's lock and key. Lily trailed a finger down the window frame of the compartment and at that moment something caught her eye, something that made her heart soar. A few carriages up stood Orlando, dressed in a footman's uniform. Lauren noticed too, she glanced at her mistress trying not to look surprised. He was staring straight at Lily, a slight smile playing on his lips.

"What are you two looking at?" demanded Betrug sharply from the other side of the carriage.

"Oh nothing," said Lily hastily. "Nothing at all."

Chapter Twenty-Three
A CURSE IS LIFTED

It was cold and dark when Isabella woke up. She shivered under the inadequate covering, feeling confused and disoriented. Where was she? What was that smell? She lifted her head and, taking in the scene, she quickly recalled the previous evening's events.

"You should have woken me," she said sleepily, as she clambered to her feet. She brushed down her clothes which still had remnants of popcorn salt sticking to the fabric, glinting like tiny crystals in the flickering light. The fire was almost out and Isaac was gathering more rubbish with which to fuel the embers.

"You looked so peaceful," said Mrs Cosy. "Besides, I couldn't sleep anyway with Prongo snoring all night."

"I wasn't snoring!" huffed the fork indignantly. "I breathe loudly that's all!"

"Anyway Isaac awoke early as well, didn't you my dear?"

Isaac nodded and shrugged, "I'm used to surviving on very little sleep, besides we don't know what's ahead of us."

Isabella stretched and yawned, "Well, thanks. Let me give you a hand."

She started to collect the remains of the old newspapers and stack them onto the flames. "Listen, about what I said last night…"

Isaac turned to her. "We were both tired and said stuff we shouldn't have. I know you and your friend were only trying to help me, and I *am* grateful."

"And I know it's not your fault we're lost – these sewers are like a maze!" she extended her hand to him. "Friends?"

Isaac smiled and shook her hand. "Sure, why not! Apart from the Magic Cutlery and the rats, I've never had any other friends."

"So what do we do now?" said Isabella.

"We wait, I suppose," he replied shrugging his shoulders.

"Are Scoopy and Shiner still sleeping?" she asked Mrs Cosy.

"Yes, my dear," said the teapot, "we'll let them sleep for the time being. You know what youngsters are like – they'll only get restless if we have a long wait in front of us."

"Yes, I suppose you're right."

They all huddled back round the fire, trying to keep warm.

"I'm hungry," sniffed Prongo after a while. "If I don't get anything to eat soon I'll begin to feel faint! There's a strong chance I will pass out!"

"You're a piece of cutlery for heavens sake! Forks aren't supposed to eat!"

"Well none of us would normally talk either but we do…beside I am an integral part of the feeding process…all you do is carry tea!"

"How dare you young man…if we weren't stuck together I'd give you what for!" said Mrs Cosy crossly.

"Please stop fighting," said Isaac. "It won't get us anywhere."

They all lapsed into silence, watching the flames twisting like ballet dancers in the damp air.

"What happens if nobody comes?" asked Isabella after a while. "I suppose we shall have to try our luck in the boat again."

"I'm not going out there again," said Prongo. "You might have a death wish but I don't want to get wet and rusty!"

"I agree, it will be too dangerous – we don't know where we are going. We were lucky no one was hurt last time. Someone will come, I know they will. The rats are always patrolling the sewers," said Isaac.

"Well that settles it then," agreed Mrs Cosy cheerily. "I have faith in young Isaac."

Isaac chewed at his fingers nervously, staring at his feet. Isabella found herself staring at him.

"Do you mind if I ask you something?" she said at last.

"It depends."

"Have you always been like that? I mean, were your parents like you as well…"

Isaac looked up sharply. "Like some deformed monster! Is that what you mean?"

"I'm sorry…I just wondered…there are so many strange creatures…er, people…and things about Zartarbia that I have not come across yet…" Isabella's voice trailed off.

"I'm not a creature, I'm a child like you…I have feelings you know! How would you like to lose both of your parents and have a curse placed upon you by the person who was supposed to care for you! My stepmother did this to me! That's why I am this way! How would you like to be locked up and treated like a slave, forced to work all the time…never allowed to play…trapped in a body that is not yours? What would you know…you're normal!" He buried his head in his hands.

Isabella got up and went to put an arm round him. "I had no idea. I'm really sorry. Please, I didn't mean to upset you."

"I'm not upset, I've just got something in my eye that's all," he said jerking his body away from her, as he fiercely wiped his eyes with a dirty bandage that was wrapped around his bony wrist.

"Alright…whatever you say," said Isabella backing off. "Is there anyway of breaking the curse? Maybe I could help? This locket…it has a powerful magic inside it…"

"I doubt it."

"It's The Locket of Fire and Water. It's how I was able to enter Zartarbia from my world. We could try. What did your stepmother do when she placed this curse on you?"

"How do you mean?"

"The curse - was it spoken? Did she touch you? Did she make you drink some potion…describe exactly what happened."

"I don't know if I can remember. I don't want to think about it."

"Come on try! How can I help you if you won't help yourself!" said Isabella sternly. "Start at the beginning."

"Well after my mother died, my father was heartbroken. We both were…we loved her so much…" began Isaac with difficulty. Nobody had ever asked him about this before, so he had always just bottled up his feelings. But once he'd started, he suddenly realised it felt good to let it all out, and the words started tumbling out.

"Go on," said Isabella lowering the tone of her voice.

"The hotel used to belong to my parents. My mother used to cook and when she died she passed her gift onto me. Father couldn't work properly. He was consumed with grief. The business was falling to pieces. Madame Glittergold was a distant cousin and she offered to run things for him. She seemed alright at first. Father was lonely and after a while she persuaded him to marry her. She moved in with her horrible son Malveo…that's when things began to change," he sniffed again, picking at his fingers.

"So what happened?"

"My father told her one day about my gift, with the cooking, that

I had got it from my mother and said what a wonderful person she had been. My stepmother flew into a terrible rage and forbade us from speaking my mother's name again. From then on, her attitude towards me changed overnight. It was as if I was a constant reminder of my mother and she was so jealous of her. The jealousy turned into a poison, she even tried to turn my own father against me and when he wouldn't listen she made his life a living hell too. Finally he couldn't take it anymore, he was exhausted with life. One morning I went to wake him and there he was lying dead on his bed, not moving, not breathing...she had finally broken him."

"How terrible!" exclaimed Isabella looking horrified.

"That was just the beginning, on the day of the burial she banished me to the kitchen and said I had to work for her or she would throw me out onto the streets. I was only eight years old. She taunted me most days and encouraged Malveo to do the same. One night I tried to escape and as punishment she placed this curse on me. She branded me with a magic amulet...see here's the mark it left," he winced as he touched the top of his left arm, pushing back the fur so that Isabella could see.

"As soon as it touched me I became...well, what I am now..."

"There, there lad...you mustn't upset yourself," said Mrs Cosy soothingly.

"At least let me try to reverse the curse," Isabella said, taking the locket from round her neck and gently placing it against the brand mark on his skin.

"Do you feel anything?" Isabella asked.

"Yes...a strange tingling," said Isaac his large eyes blinking with surprise.

Almost straight away, the fur on Isaac's skin started to fade, as if the locket was sucking in his monstrous form. Within a matter of moments, a pale boy of thirteen years of age emerged, his horrific disguise banished. He looked at his hands and then down at his feet in disbelief.

"It worked!" shouted Isabella in excitement. "Look, Mrs Cosy! Prongo! Look!"

"Well I never," said the teapot smiling. "It's a miracle! Oh my dear boy, quick, have a look at yourself in the water."

Gingerly Isaac got up and walked over to the water. He crouched down and peered at his reflection, touching his face.

"I don't believe it!" he whispered in wonderment, seeing a face that he hadn't seen in a long time.

"Hey Scoopy and Shiner! Wake up, come quickly and see Isaac!" shouted Prongo.

"What is it? What's going on?" said the two little teaspoons, in dazed, sleepy voices.

"Isaac is a boy again! The curse has gone! I'm so happy, I think I'm going to cry," said the fork, blowing his metal nose on a corner of the handkerchief sail.

Isaac hugged Isabella. "I don't know how to thank you!"

"There's no need. That's what friends are for."

Within moments they were all jumping in the air, cheering and whooping. They danced around, singing at the tops of their voices and clapping their hands.

Chapter Twenty-Four
VOYAGE TO THE RAT KINGDOM

"Ahoy 'dere!" shouted a voice in the distance. "What's all der noise about?"

They all spun round, to see a small boat heading towards them with a rat carrying a lantern.

"It's a patrol boat. We're saved!" said Isaac breathlessly. "We're over here!" he shouted waving his arms.

"Well I can see dat, can't I or I would no 'ave called to you! Is you friend or foe?" shouted the furry creature.

"I'm a friend of King Pizarro!" yelled Isaac. "Can you take us to him…we have some important business to discuss with him!"

"How do I know you no lying? You might be bandits tryin' to trick me, eh? You might cut off my tail and steal my boat!"

"We're not lying!" shouted Isabella. "Please we just want to see the king…we've just escaped from the Hotel Gastronomic…we really need you help!"

The rat scratched his head. "Well, I don' know!"

"Look, we have our own boat…why would we want to steal yours? We just need you to guide us to the Kingdom of Discarded Treasure and Water."

"Ah ha!" said the rat brandishing a sword fashioned from toothpicks. "So dat is your game? You after der king's treasure…upon my honour, I shall die first, I shall defend der king…you have to torture me before I tell you where 'is majesty is!"

"No, we don't want his treasure, we just need to talk to him…please help us!" said Isaac.

"Even if you singe my ears and clip my claws, you get nada from me!" said the rat dramatically, as if he had not heard the boy's last comment.

"I have an idea," said Isabella, quickly rummaging in the rubbish for the small ladies purse. "See. It has some coins in it…tell him we have brought a gift for the king."

"Señor Rat?" shouted Isaac. "We come with a present for the king – Mira! Un regalo. Look, I have it here…surely that is proof enough!"

The rat eyed him suspiciously.

"Sir… I used to save food for your fellow comrades, for the king himself!"

"OK, Vale…I decide to trust you eh! But any trickiness and I run you t'rough with my sword, comprende?"

"Comprendo!" said Isaac.

The rat guided his boat over to them, which upon closer inspection was made from an old shoe.

"What call ya'self?" asked the rat, as he jumped nimbly down onto the ground.

"This is Isabella, Mrs Cosy, Prong, Scoopy and Shiner and I'm Isaac," said the boy. "Encantado, Señor."

"You speaka da Spanish, uh?" said the rat, looking bemused.

"Solo un poco. Just the few words that King Pizarro has taught me."

"Soy Pedro," said the rat extending a paw. "Now we must maka da haste" and with that he tied one of the shoe laces from his boat round Mrs Cosy's spout.

"Not too tight, please," instructed the teapot.

"Eh Señora…we do it my way or no way! Now give me da present and we get going."

Isaac handed him the purse, which the rat quickly sniffed before opening it up, his beady eyes lighting up at the sight of the gold coins. Isaac and Isabella gently pushed Mrs Cosy into the water and picked up Scoopy and Shiner.

"Rapido amigos, da tide will soon to turn. We go now…vamos!" shouted the rat.

Within moments they were once again sailing through the complex maze of sewers.

It seemed an age before they reached The Kingdom of Discarded Treasure and Water. Despite a few attempts at conversation with the rat, the creature remained wary of them as he led them through the murky water towards the palace. As they drew nearer, Isabella could see the palace was constructed from an array of cardboard boxes, postcards, old paperback books and comics, all held together quite neatly with tape, drawing pins and clips. There were turrets made from small tasselled lampshades and crystal drinking glasses that had been turned upside down. In front of the palace was an old painted fireguard surrounded by fairy lights, with a grand doorway that had been cut, or chewed, out in the middle (for it is a well known fact that rats are exceedingly good at gnawing through almost anything). A pair of goggles, some horn rimmed spectacles and various pieces of car head lights formed the windows.

Isabella found herself feeling most surprised that these rats had such imagination and were so resourceful. Now she understood why Pedro called it the Kingdom of Discarded Treasure and Water. They moored the boats and Pedro shouted. "Eh, Carlos…lower der drawbridge! We got visitors, one of dem claims to know King Pizarro, says dey amigos…"

"Que? What you say Pedro?" shouted a distant voice as a head popped out of one of the turrets.

"Open up!…dey bring regalo for Rey Pizarro…let us in, hombre!"

The drawbridge (which was made from a small tray and a couple of tape measures) was duly lowered and they entered. A group of rat soldiers quickly lifted Mrs Cosy and the others onto a skateboard and wheeled them inside.

The inside of the palace was truly amazing and very ingenious. They were led through a great hallway fashioned from several old suitcases and a fur coat. Walls were decorated with stamps and sweet wrappers. A portrait of the king was painted on a piece of driftwood and hung at the end of the hall. The floors were constructed from bits of broken tile and jigsaw pieces. Curtains were made from frilly knickers and string vests, pegged to coat hangers.

Pedro duly took them to a grand salon where King Pizarro was sitting in an ornate sugar bowl that had been chipped away to form a throne. Two tiny bells were tied by gold and purple ribbon to the handles either side. The king was dressed in a magnificent costume sewn from tiny scraps of ornate fabric and on his head he wore a crown created from beads, buttons, dismantled rings and wire. Behind him, a lady's vanity mirror had been fixed high upon the wall and various candlesticks were placed around the room. Instead of statues, an odd assortment of objects adorned the hall – a plastic dinosaur, some fake flowers, a telephone and a magnifying glass.

Pedro went up to the king, bowed deeply and handed him the purse they had found. He whispered something in his ear. King Pizarro nodded and gestured for them to come forwards. Isaac

King Pizarro
and
Captain
Miguel

went over to him bowing deeply, closely followed by Isabella.

"Your Majesty, thank you for seeing us."

The king stroked his whiskers quizzically. "So what can I do for you? You claim we are amigos, but how can dat be when I don' recognise you?"

"It's a long story, Sir," he replied. "But I am Isaac, the rat boy….the last time I saw Capitán Miguel, he brought me some presents that you sent - a book and a hot water bottle. I would save scraps of food for you…at the Hotel Gastronomic, don't you remember?"

"What is my favourite food den?"

Isaac smiled, "That's easy…you love fish baked in salt…in particular dorada, and prawns cooked in olive oil and garlic…and you like the way I make tortilla..."

"Bastante! Es verdad, si is true!" the king stood up and embraced Isaac. "Welcome amigo…so what happened?"

"The curse has been lifted…my friend Isabella, she has a magic locket…see," he said, pointing to the Locket of Fire and Water.

King Pizarro lifted a furry eyebrow. "I hear rumours of dis locket…you come from da otro world 'den señorita? Ah, how interesting!" said the King, sucking in his breath sharply. "Eh Capitán Miguel, come look at dis. The girl has da locket… she come from another world…"

"Pleased to make your acquaintance," said Isabella curtseying.

"Be seated, por favor. Make yourselves at home – mi casa es tu casa," said the king smiling broadly. "Bring refreshments for our guests!"

Capitán Miguel slapped Isaac on the back. "Eh, amigo, I no recognise you…you gotta new look eh? I no sure, no se…I like when you more hairy. An' you so small now too?"

Isaac smiled, "The size is only temporary, but I am glad to have got rid of the hair. Anyhow, it's good to see you Capitán."

"Eh well si' down, hombre, and tell us all, uh!"

The children sat down, Isaac on a chair that had been fashioned out of a cigar box and was lined with shredded toilet paper and Isabella on another made from a coconut shell cushioned with bubblewrap.

"So tell me, what I can do for you?" said the king.

Isabella was handed a thimble filled to the brim with some delicious fizzy liquid, whilst Isaac was given a toothpaste cap to drink from.

Over the next few hours they explained everything including their concerns about Oro Cazador.

"Si! I know of dis man, he has da glass eye, no?" exclaimed King Pizarro.

"Yes, we think he has been planning something terrible for Zartarbia…my friend Agent Lujzka she was fairly sure it had something to with Isaac and his special talent. She works for the FADF and I have tried to contact them but I don't know if the message has reached them."

"I see. Well we need, how you say, a plan of action….let me consult con Capitán Miguel. In der meantime, you get sleep…you must be tired."

Isabella yawned. "Sorry, yes we are… it's been a long journey. Can you get word to the FADF headquarters, in case the hologram I sent hasn't arrived. I want to make sure Lujzka's alright."

"Si, Señorita, we take care of dis. Now Maria will show you to your quarters."

Isabella woke up many hours later with a sinking feeling in the pit of her stomach. She had dreamt of the Dungeon of Skeletons again and amidst the bones, she had seen Lujzka. She crawled out of her bed which was a pencil case padded with cotton wool, and pushed aside the face towel that covered her. Though the room was pleasantly warm and a candle burned brightly, she felt chilly inside. There was a knock on the door and a maid came in.

"Hola, Señorita Isabella. I have run hot bath for you and I bring you new clothes."

"Oh…erm, that really wasn't necessary but thank you anyway. I wonder if I might see the king?" said Isabella politely.

The maid smiled kindly. "Oh no, dat is no possible ahora. Der King and Capitán Miguel stay up verra late discussing matters; he no appreciate being disturbed just yet. Ven. Come an' have dat bath. I take you to 'is majesty later, OK?"

"Alright then," agreed Isabella reluctantly.

It was some time later before they were all summoned for breakfast which (it had to be said) was not particularly appetising. Stale bread had been soaked in some tepid milk and bacon rind had been added into the mix, along with some soggy cabbage leaves. Isabella, who did not wish to appear rude, tried to swallow a couple of mouthfuls but found it quite disgusting.

King Pizarro, on the other hand, was eating his meal heartily.

"Es muy bueno uh?" he said shovelling another mouthful in. "Eh why you no eat?"

"I'm not hungry that's all," said Isabella, smiling un-convincingly.

"You no like?" asked the king after he had polished off the rest of his breakfast and then eaten the bowl it was in too.

"Actually, I am too worried to eat," began Isabella, relieved to be able to tell the King of her doubts.

"Tell me!" said King Pizarro.

"My friend Lujzka, you know the FADF agent I told you about?…Well I think that she is in trouble …I have no proof but I dreamt last night that she was in danger ."

"I see," said the king slowly. "Last night I dispatch soldiers to

FADF but is a verra long journey, eh, so they no return yet. Also, I send some of my spies to der Hotel Gastronomic...your – how do you say, um, premonition was correct. I regret I have der bad news for you. Dey get back dis morning and der information suggest your friend is ...muerte."

"Muerte?...I don't understand."

"Er...she is dead."

"No! I don't believe it!" cried Isabella. "It can't be true!"

"I afraid it is, Señorita Isabella. Dey bring dis as proof," he said, snapping his fingers at two rats who carried in a long metal key on their shoulders. They set it down in front of her.

"Jangle!" exclaimed Isabella. "What happened?"

The key shook his head. "It was terrible. I saw it with my own eyes! That Transcender..."

"Betrug Espion?"

"Yes. He carried off her lifeless body and there was nothing I could do, I just lay on the floor watching him take her away!"

"Are you sure she was dead?" said Isabella, numb with shock.

The key nodded. "I'm sorry Isabella...I am certain..."

"My condolences, Señorita," said the king gravely.

Isabella buried her head in her hands, sobbing uncontrollably. The table fell silent.

Chapter Twenty-Five
JET BLACK ARRIVES

The journey to Segregaria passed by uneventfully and in due course everybody was scanned into the castle. Oro Cazador watched Malveo carefully, wondering how such a repellent and seemingly stupid boy could be capable of creating such stupendous food. The boy wandered around the kitchen looking disinterested and bored.

"Do you like your new kitchen? It has everything you should need," said Oro. "Your mother brought it all from Sumptitious."

"Pumpkin, it's wonderful, isn't it?" trilled Dorian Glittergold, jabbing him in the back to urge him to be at least interested. "So much bigger than the one we had at the hotel!"

"It's alright," shrugged Malveo, stifling a yawn.

"Oh, don't mind him," she said brightly, linking her arm through Oro's, "he's just a little tired, that's all. It's been so much to take in. After all, the past few days have been somewhat of a whirlwind, haven't they? Besides, Malveo will need all his energy for the big day tomorrow."

"Indeed," said Oro gruffly, "I'm expecting great things from you, young man. Make your mother and me proud."

Malveo opened a fridge, taking out a large cream cake. "I'll try," he said indifferently, before stuffing the whole thing in his mouth.

"Well, my dear lady. I have matters of business to attend to, so I will wish you goodnight," he said, kissing her hand.

"Of course, my beloved, whatever you say – until tomorrow then!" she tittered.

Oro marched off towards his private study where he found Lily was waiting with Lauren.

"It is late my, dear, why are you still up?" he scowled. "I told the maid to escort you to your room."

"Sorry Sir, it's just that mi'lady said it was urgent she spoke to you before she retired for the evening," said Lauren anxiously. "She was most insistent, Sir."

"Papa, I made her promise to let me wait so I could talk with you," interrupted Lily, kissing her father on the cheek. "I told her you would be most displeased if you didn't hear what I have to say tonight."

"Well, a few more minutes won't hurt," he said looking at his watch. Turning to Lauren he instructed, "You wait for my daughter upstairs. She will be along presently."

Lauren curtsied and fled from the room.

"What is it that's so important, Lily?"

"It's about your marriage to Madame Glittergold," she said carefully, watching him pour himself a drink.

"What about it?" he said abruptly.

"I should like to get to know her a little better and her two cousins, after all if we are to be a family I think it would be nice to spend some time with them. I thought I could help with some of the wedding arrangements."

"That won't be necessary. You know we have plenty of staff to do that sort of thing. You don't need to get those pretty hands of yours all dirty and sore with housework."

"I know, but I thought it would be a nice gesture if I did something myself. I thought I could ask Lady Dee and Lady Dah if they would like to organise the flower arrangements with me."

"Your sentiment is admirable, my dear, but I'm not sure…"

"Oh please Papa, I just want to have a part in the marriage tomorrow, that's all. I mean, Madame Glittergold's son is preparing the banquet and I would like to play my part too, even if it is just a small one. It would make me so happy!"

"Alright Lily, if you want to you can, on one condition, that they never let you out of their sight."

"Oh! Thank you, Papa," she said throwing her arms around his neck. "I shall ask Lauren to order the flowers first thing tomorrow."

He smiled, stroking her hair. "Well, off to bed then."

Lily ran up the stairs of the tower and for the first time in her life she didn't feel dismayed by the sound of her father locking the door behind her.

She burst into her room and ran up to Lauren, who was stroking a small bird.

"He's agreed! All you have to do is ask Orlando to bring the flowers in and then leave the rest to me."

"I still can't believe he followed you. He must really love you to have taken such a big risk," Lauren murmured, wishing some young man would go to the ends of the earth for her.

"I know. I can't wait to see him again! I shall send him a note now to let him know the good news."

The atmosphere in The Kingdom of Discarded Treasure and Water had been most subdued since the news of Lujzka's death. Isabella had been inconsolable and had spent the entire day in her room crying. She refused to speak to anybody, not even Isaac.

King Pizarro and Capitán Miguel were in deep discussions when the rat messengers they had sent to Securical returned accompanied by two FADF agents, Jet Black and Blaze Strike (both who had been shrunk using the same device Lujzka had used with Isabella and Isaac).

Jet swept into the Great Hall, bowing low to the king.

"Your Majesty, I am Jet Black and this is my associate Blaze Strike - on behalf of the FADF I would like to thank your prompt help in the matter of the human girl, and for keeping her safe. Though she is just a child, she possesses great powers that could change the course of Zartarbian history forever."

"Eh, you never would to guess but I glad to assist, hombre."

"I must speak to Isabella as soon as possible, on a matter most urgent. Where is she?"

"She most upset by der death of her friend…what is der girl's name?"

Capitán Miguel whispered something in his ear. "Si, dat it! Lujzka, she was an agent too, si?"

"I don't know where you got your information from, but she's not dead."

The king pointed to Jangle. "But dis one here, he said he sec everything!"

"I did! I saw her body at the Hotel Gastronomic. She was dead," said the key defensively. "That Transcender spy was carrying her!"

Jet shook his head. "No, he had simply knocked her out. Every FADF agent has one of these," he said, pulling back a flap of skin on his arm and revealing a series of small electronic buttons. "We received a coded message from her just hours ago – she was able to give us details of where she is being held."

"I see," said the king, stroking his whiskers. "Maria! Go and fetch Señorita Isabella immediately."

"Detective Valise, head of the FADF, has asked me to give you this," said Jet.

King Pizarro opened the letter.

'Your Majesty

Firstly I hope I find you in good health as it has been a long time since I last had the honour of your company. I thank you for keeping Isabella Zophie and Isaac safely under your protection.

I must, however, request one further favour from you. Two of our agents have been captured by The Syndicate member Oro Cazador, and are being held at Segregaria.

It is a place that is almost impossible to penetrate but it has been brought to my attention that you may know a secret way in and I should like to ask for your help in this matter. I have sent two of my best agents who will know exactly what to do once inside Cazador's castle, but we need you to show them the way in.

My old friend - I hope I can count on your support

Yours faithfully

Detective Frederick Valise'

King Pizarro glanced at Capitán Miguel. "Vale! We know it can be done but der problem is der security arrangements, dey keep to change! Tis muy difícil."

"Es verdad! It won't be easy, but we try!"

"Si, Si! We try, eh! Ah and here is Señorita Isabella," he said as she rushed into the room throwing herself at Jet.

"Hey, steady! Where's the fire?!" he laughed, catching her.

"Is it true? Is Lujzka really alive?" Isabella gulped, her eyes lit up with hope.

"Yes, but she is in serious danger."

"Has Cazador got her?" she asked anxiously, remembering what

Lujzka had said about him being utterly ruthless.

"Yes, and he has Agent Chloe as well. We have to get them out of Segregaria as soon as possible. His Majesty has very graciously agreed to help us, but we must leave straight away."

"I want to come too. She risked her life to save mine and Isaac's."

"No, Detective Valise gave me strict instructions. You and Isaac were to be escorted to Securical."

"Well, I'm not going!" said Isabella stubbornly.

"Neither me," said Isaac. "She's right. Lujzka is in trouble because of us, because she tried to help me!"

"I'm sorry but Monsieur Valise…" began Jet, who had never thought for a moment that Isabella would meekly walk away from helping to rescue Lujzka. She was far too spirited. And he was right.

Isabella and Isaac stood side by side, their expressions defying Jet. "We're coming with you," they said, arms folded.

"Good! Because I might well need you," Jet agreed readily defying his boss' commands. "But we have to leave now! King Pizarro, do you have any maps that show how we could possibly access Cazador's castle?"

Chapter Twenty-Six
A GHOSTLY WARNING

Dorian had just finished putting curlers in her hair, when Malveo entered.

"I'm worried about tomorrow," he whined, feeling most sorry for himself.

"There's nothing to be worried about," she said, patting the chair next to her. "You have the magic cutlery…"

"But they're ignoring me mummykins," said Malveo sullenly.

"You just need to bully them a bit, darling," his mother replied, tweaking his chubby cheeks. 'They'll soon get the message, you just have to show them who is boss. Have a yummy chocolate to keep your energy up, and you will feel better," she said offering him a large box. He started to eat his way through the first layer.

"After tomorrow is over, my little pumpkin, we won't have to keep up the pretence. Oro isn't going to expect you to cook every night as he's got an army of staff for that. It's a symbolic gesture, that's all."

"I don't like him. He's talking about me going into the family business."

"But that's a good thing! Now, darling, I admit he is different from your last step-father but you just need to get used to him.

He's really quite amiable… although you have to understand powerful men are used to getting their own way. We shall simply need to accommodate his occasional mood swings which is a small price to pay for a lifetime of luxury…and besides, you want mummykins to be happy don't you?" she said, contorting her face into a fake pout.

Malveo looked at her, sighing. "It's just that there's something really weird about him."

She patted his hand. "That will be his glass eye. It's disconcerting I know but not everybody can be as handsome as my precious boy. Now, it is late. Run along to bed – tomorrow is going to be very busy, pumpkin."

Malveo nodded reluctantly.

"There's a good boy," she said, kissing him on both cheeks. "We'll be fine snogglepops, don't worry."

As soon as he'd gone, Dorian took out the necklace that Oro had given her, admiring the fine quality of the gems. Tootles was quietly snuffling in the corner of the bedroom, already asleep. Madame Glittergold gave him a little pat and pulled the covers over him before getting into her own bed.

Dorian was just about to fall asleep when she realised she was not alone.

Three ghosts had suddenly appeared and were sitting on her bed!

One was middle-aged in appearance and wore a padded night gown, another was a young blond woman dressed in a baby doll nightie and the third had her hair in curlers and was wrapped up in a fluffy bathrobe.

"So you're the next Mrs Cazador," said the middle-aged ghost raising her eyebrow. "Well we thought it only fair to warn you about him."

"I'm dreaming. This is just a dream," said Dorian shutting her eyes and opening them again, fully expecting the room to be empty.

"If only you were darling, but that's men for you – can't be trusted eh?" said the blond one as she filed her nails.

"Who are you?" said Dorian trembling as she clutched the covers to her neck.

"Oh sorry, how rude! I'm Edie," she said, "and this is Maureen and Gertrude. We're all previous Mrs Cazadors you see. Oh look she's wearing the ring!"

Dorian nervously twisted the diamond on her finger. "I don't understand."

"Ah bless! Well of course you don't understand," said Edie. "That's why we're here darling - to explain the situation."

"Yes, you see we've all been where you are now, he's given that ring to each of us," said Gertrude as she started to take the curlers out of her hair. "I mean I know he's not much to look at but he's quite a ladies man if you know what I mean. We all fell for his charms only to realise we'd married a monster!"

"What are you talking about?"

"Our husband of course!" said Maureen matter of factly. "I was his third wife. He bumped me off on our honeymoon, pretended I'd run off with a sailor – the cheek of it! As if I'd stoop so low! I came from an aristocratic family."

"Oh, don't be such a snob!" tutted Edie as she picked up some of Dorian's perfume and casually squirted herself with it. "I really don't know what he ever saw in you to begin with!"

"Class and breeding my dear, something that you wouldn't know anything about!" snapped the middle aged ghost.

"Oh stop it you two!" said Gertrude. "Let's just finish the warning. Now listen dear," she said wagging her hairbrush at Dorian. "If you marry Oro, you will end up like us, mark my words."

"I don't believe you! This is a nightmare!" said Dorian shaking.

"You can say that again darling!" said Edie. "How do you think we feel, stuck in limbo like this!"

"Leave me alone! You're lying!" shrieked Dorian.

"Well that's gratitude for you! We've interrupted our slumber party to deliver this warning!" said the young ghost pouting.

"She's in denial. Well we tried," sighed Gertrude. "What number will that make her?"

"The one hundred and fifty fourth, I believe," replied Maureen irritably. "Well no matter. I for one have better things to do with my time than count the amount of wives Oro's got through! I've some knitting to get back to."

"Come on girls, we're clearly wasting our time here," said Edie, "all this haunting is boring me to tears. Let's get back, if we hurry we can catch the end of that soap opera."

And with that they were gone, leaving Dorian wondering if she had imagined the whole thing.

Chapter Twenty-Seven
A ROMANCE BLOSSOMS

Dorian Glittergold awoke the following morning feeling distinctly uneasy. She tried to convince herself she had just imagined the ghostly warning but something kept niggling away inside her. She immediately summoned her cousins.

"What is it now, Dorian?" said Lady Dee, a look of sleepy exasperation on her face. Really her cousin had become so neurotic, she thought to herself.

"Did you not sleep well?" added Lady Dah, pulling her silk dressing gown around her.

"Something very strange happened last night," said Madame Glittergold anxiously looking behind her and then back again.

"You have pre-wedding jitters! It's only natural, my dear," said Lady Dee.

"Yes. After all, today's your big day!" said her sister, patting Dorian's hand.

"No, it's not that…well, maybe I'm a little nervous but I received a warning last night," said Dorian, lowering her voice dramatically.

"A warning?" asked Lady Dee, looking at her quizzically.

"Who from?" chipped in Lady Dah.

"It's going to sound like madness, but I think I saw a ghost. She said I would be killed by Oro and that I had to get away from this place before it was too late!"

"Oh Dorian! You are a hoot!" snorted Lady Dah.

"Yes, my dear, that's quite preposterous," smirked her sister.

"It all seemed very real… there were others too. They all claimed to have been married to him and said he had murdered them. They said they wanted to warn me," replied Dorian, beginning to doubt herself.

"Piffle!" said Lady Dee firmly. "You imagined it. Ghosts don't exist! Everybody knows that."

"You had a nightmare that's all. Surely you can't believe he's capable of such terrible deeds," admonished Lady Dah

"No, of course not!" Dorian said, then hesitated. "Although he has a bit of a temper, a dark side even…"

"But murder, cousin dear, that's ridiculous!" exclaimed Lady Dee.

"Yes, you're right I suppose," said Dorian feeling rather foolish.

"Of course we are," said Lady Dee authoritatively.

"You have more important things to attend to," finished Lady Dah brightly.

"And we must make tracks." Lady Dee tapped the face of her watch, looking at her sister.

"Lily Rose has asked to meet us. She wants us to help with some of the wedding arrangements. That's nice, isn't it?" cooed Lady Dah.

"She said she wanted to be involved personally, to get to know us as a family and she would hardly do that if her father was planning on murdering us all!" laughed Lady Dee. "You must put this nonsense from your thoughts."

"And we shall see you later," said Lady Dee.

"Okay," agreed Dorian, beginning to feel better. "Can you knock on Malveo's door on your way down. I don't want him oversleeping. He needs to get that magic cutlery working, as it was being quite unhelpful last night and I am sure he is a little behind."

"Of course, cousin dear," said Lady Dee air-kissing her cheek.

Lily Rose was so excited that she could barely contain herself, as she waited for the two sisters. Glace watched her suspiciously and then glanced at her watch. "Well I hope they get here soon as I can't leave you until they arrive."

"I'm sure they'll be along in a moment," said Lily, peering out of the window.

"I don't know what you've got to be so happy about, anyway? Your father is only getting married again," Glace sniffed, looking down her nose at her niece.

"I'm just pleased for Papa. It's nice to see him happy."

"I doubt it will last long," Glace snorted.

"Why do you say that?"

"Because they never do. Enduring relationships are not your father's strong point. Wives just clutter up the place and get in the way of important matters like business."

Lily ignored her, feeling blissfully happy inside in anticipation of seeing Orlando again.

"Sorry, we're late!" trilled Lady Dee and Lady Dah as they breezed into the room.

"About time too!" snapped Glace. "Now you're not to let her out of your sight, understood!"

"Of course."

"We understand," they chorused.

"Good. Well, I have things to do!" she said marching out like a dark shadow.

"My, my, she's not exactly friendly, is she?" said Lady Dee, when Glace was safely out of earshot.

"Oh don't mind her, she's always like that," Lily said.

"So what would you like us to do?" asked the sisters.

"I thought we might arrange the flowers together. My maid has just gone to tell the footmen to fetch them."

"Right then, well, this will be fun… not that we actually know anything about flower arranging!" simpered Lady Dah.

"We'll give it a whirl though! All girls together!" giggled Lady Dee.

Lauren appeared at the doorway, closely followed by five footmen, including Orlando. Lily thought she would explode when they exchanged glances, but both had to maintain the pretence that they didn't know each other. Orlando's fingers brushed against hers as he laid the flowers out, and Lily blushed furiously. However the two sisters seemed oblivious to any change in the atmosphere.

"Perhaps I should ask one of the footman to stay and help us with the arrangements," said Lily as casually as she could. "I mean, if flower arranging is not your strongest point, then I know this footman is particularly skilled," she said, pointing casually to her lover. The twin sisters nodded their agreement, and the rest of the footmen left. They all carried on sorting through flowers, picking them up and sniffing them.

"Oh! Smell this one!" said Lily, putting a large rose under the sister's noses.

"Oh, that smells delightful," said Lady Dah, before sneezing violently all of a sudden.

"Quite divine!" agreed Lady Dee, before her eyes started to water furiously.

"Oh dear! I don't know what is wrong!" exclaimed Lady Dah blowing her nose loudly.

"Achoo! I think we may have an allergy to these blooms!" said Lady Dee, sneezing again.

"Yes, the effect they are having does seem quite potent," agreed her sister.

"Well if they are causing you discomfort then maybe we could meet up later. After all we have plenty of time to get to know each other better," said Lily, trying to look concerned (although she knew full well that Orlando had put a strong sneezing powder all over the rose).

"Well, if you don't mind," said Lady Dah.

"I'm quite sure, besides I'm sure Madame Glittergold needs your help more. I have plenty of staff to assist me and I'm sure you don't want to be sneezing throughout the ceremony this evening."

"Oh but we can't leave you alone. We were told we mustn't!" sniffed Lady Dee suddenly.

"I'll be fine. My aunt is a little over-protective that's all. I am in no danger here as Segregaria has the best security system in Zartarbia."

"I'm not so sure," said Lady Dee, remembering Glace's warning.

"I'm fine," Lily paused, "but, oh dear, your noses have gone quite red!"

(Orlando had also put a dye into the roses.)

Both sisters looked at each other in horror and fled. They couldn't possibly go to a wedding tonight with their appearances being as they were.

Lily and Orlando grinned conspiratorially at each other. They were finally alone whilst Lauren kept watch at the door.

"I can't believe you followed me! You're risking your life…if my father knew you were here!"

"I couldn't let you go! I love you!" said Orlando kissing her.

"I love you too. Listen, we don't have much time. I think I know how we can be together but it will be extremely dangerous."

"I would do anything for you."

"We will have to run away and keep running. It's the only way. There can be no turning back, my father will try to hunt us down and, if he catches us, he will certainly kill you."

"If I can't be with you then it will be as if I am dead anyway."

"There is a secret passage that Papa doesn't think I know about. Once the wedding banquet is served, I shall slip away on the pretext of fetching a gift for my father. I know where he keeps the key. I will meet you back here and then we shall elope together," she said urgently.

"Are you absolutely certain that this is what you want?"

"Yes, more than anything else."

"Quick! Someone is coming!" whispered Lauren loudly, peeping through a crack in the door.

"Until this evening, my love!" said Orlando and with that, he was gone.

Chapter Twenty-Eight
THE MAGIC CUTLERY

The sneezing fits that Lady Dee and Lady Dah had experienced stopped as quickly as it had started and after washing their faces, the allergic reaction to their noses also disappeared. They re-powdered their faces and were just heading towards their sleeping quarters when Malveo came racing down the corridor covered in flour, a broken egg dripping from his hair. "Quickly! You must fetch Mama!"

"Whatever is the matter?" squeaked Lady Dah, clutching her sister's arm.

"THEY keep attacking me!" howled the boy.

"Right, go back to the kitchen and wait for us there!" instructed Lady Dee. "We'll inform your mother."

Madame Glittergold entered the kitchen, flanked by Lady Dee and Lady Dah. The kitchen was in total disarray and Malveo had his podgy face in a bowl of jam. Dorian pursed her lips and folded her arms across her ample chest.

"WHAT is going on, Malveo?" she said sternly.

The boy hastily lifted his head. "Mama...I was hungry..."

"No, not that. Why isn't the feast prepared? Have you any idea how angry Oro is going to be? He asked this one small thing of you, *I* asked this one small thing of you - my only son."

Her podgy son shook his head, accidentally wiping a streak of raspberry jam across his cheek. "It's not my fault. THEY won't help me. THEY say they're on strike…please don't be angry with me. I've tried, I really have!"

"He's nothing more than a lazy lump, a spoilt brat," said Mrs Pan in disgust.

Dorian turned round sharply. "Who dares insult my precious pumpkin?"

The Magic Cutlery huddled together, watching her defiantly.

"Oh mummykins, it was awful…I'm so glad you're here – now you can see how horrid they are to me," he snuffled, pulling a face.

"Come here," said Dorian embracing her son. "It's alright, I'm here…I'll sort this out. I'm sorry. I shouldn't have shouted at you."

"They were so nasty to me," sobbed Malveo, playing on his mother's sympathy. Lady Dee and Lady Dah rolled their eyes in unison, fed up with their nephew's manipulative behaviour and worried that he might mess up the whole wedding. It was too important that it went off without the slightest hitch.

"Is that so? Well nobody upsets my darling boy and gets away with it!" she hissed, a steely glint in her eyes. "I'll deal with this."

Malveo nodded his head with a pained look on his face. "I tried, I really did mummykins, but …they called me names and threw eggs at me!"

"My poor, brave little soldier…you tried your best and that's all that counts."

"It's all that freak's fault. He's the one that's got us into this mess…they said they won't work for anybody but him!"

"Don't upset yourself now," said Dorian soothingly. "Why don't you run along to mummykin's room and help yourself to some more of those chocolates you like – that will cheer you up, won't it?"

Malveo sniffed again, nodding as his mother covered him in lipstick kisses. "Now off you go pumpkin."

Dorian's loving expression hardened as soon as he had departed. "Right! Which one of you tinpot troublemakers is the leader?"

"We don't have a leader, we're a dem – demo…democracy," piped up Master Porcelain, the small bowl. "That means we all make decisions together."

"I know what it means, you stupid idiot!" She advanced on the bowl and picked him up. "Open your mouth again and I'll break you!"

"Oi, leave it out!" shouted Mr Bristles (the broom), brushing her into the corner. "Threaten the lad again and you'll have me to deal with!"

"How dare you! You'll be firewood before the day's through! Let me make it clear to you all that when I say jump, you do it!" screamed Dorian, her face turning an unattractive shade of purple.

"You don't frighten me…you're nothing but a big bully!" retorted Mr Bristles.

"You can't bully US!" said Frothy, the whisk.

Dorian Glittergold was about to open her mouth and unleash a torrent of abuse when Lady Dee gently squeezed her arm.

"Cousin dear, don't distress yourself," she whispered behind her hand. "Besides we need their help…"

Madame Glittergold paused for a moment, casting a suspicious eye over the Magic Cutlery. She took a deep breath and gritted her teeth.

"Now listen to me, and listen carefully," she said. "You will co-operate or…"

"Or wot?" said Mrs Roly. "Listen luv, frets won't work."

The other members of the Magic Cutlery muttered their agreement.

"Why should we co-operate? You treated Isaac worse than a dog," said Steamy the kettle, as he bubbled away on the fire.

"If I might have a word, cousin dear," interjected Lady Dah quickly, pulling Dorian away from the madding crowd of cutlery.

The three women huddled together in the corner of the kitchen.

"We think maybe insults won't work," began Lady Dah calmly.

"Perhaps a deal can be struck…" suggested Lady Dee.

"…after all, you only need them for the wedding feast," finished Lady Dah.

"What sort of deal?" asked Dorian doubtfully.

"I don't know - talk to them, bribe them, do whatever you need to do," said Lady Dee.

"Yes, cousin dear. Once you are Oro's bride, you have no more need for them. Oro doesn't know about Isaac…" added Lady Dah.

"All we have to do is get through today," said Lady Dee.

"She's right. All you have to do is persuade them to help," urged Lady Dah.

"After tonight's feast you will have all his staff to wait on you hand and foot," murmured Lady Dee.

"But what if he expects Malveo to cook again?" said Dorian, her frown furrowed with worry. "He was saying he has great plans for him."

"He probably wants Malveo to work in his family business," said Lady Dee.

"He just wants Malveo to create the wedding feast as a symbol of your union, the joining of your two families," explained Lady Dah. "You're fretting over nothing, dear cousin. "

"Besides you can always chop off the boy's hands – that way he can't cook again and the problem is sorted," said her sister nonchalantly.

Dorian looked at her in horror. "How could you even suggest such a thing!"

"Alright maybe that was a little extreme, perhaps we just break his fingers..." shrugged Lady Dee.

"She's joking," said Lady Dah glaring at her twin.

"She'd better be! Her comments were in extremely bad taste. Anyway it doesn't help us with our present predicament – what about the Magic Cutlery?"

"Just talk to them..." Lady Dah urged, "nicely."

"You must do whatever it takes to get them to co-operate," insisted Lady Dee. Dorian nodded and walked back over to the restless semi-circle of cutlery.

"Clearly we have got off on the wrong foot," Madame Glittergold said in a sickly sweet voice.

"That's a bloomin' understatement," muttered Mrs Roly.

Dorian ignored her, "I know I have been a tad...well...unfair at times and I think the time is right for us to build bridges, for me to make amends to you all....so I'm sorry if you think that I have been a little harsh on you in the past. We must look to the future. After all, I am to be married and we shall be one big happy family...surely you can find it in your hearts to do this one thing for me..."

"You've got to be joking!" snorted Mrs Pan in disgust.

"Yeah, giv' us one good reason why we should 'elp you! 'Cause the way we see it, this is your problem not ours," said Mrs Roly crossly.

The rest of the Magic Cutlery all voiced their agreement, clattering and clinking against the kitchen work surfaces.

"Let me try," said Lady Dee pushing her cousin to one side.

"Ladies and gentlemen, you are quite right of course and naturally we would not ask this of you unless we had to. Obviously we would not expect you to do this for nothing, indeed you only have to ask for what you want and it shall be yours."

"Anything?" said Mr Bristles.

"Within reason," interspersed Dorian quickly.

"Anything," replied Lady Dee firmly, "gold, jewels, furs…anything at all – you just have to name it and it's yours."

"Wot need 'ave we for jewels an' furs?" said the rolling pin.

"Alright, what do you want? Listen! Please, at least consider our proposal. We are begging you."

Lady Dah outstretched her arms to them. "We can't do this without you, I beseech you to help us with this one thing…"

Mr Bristles turned to the others, "What do you think?"

"I don't trust any of them," said Glinty, shaking his blade at them.

"Look. Just think about it, why don't we give you a few moments to talk it over amongst yourselves…after all it is a group decision," she said sweetly, looking at Master Porcelain.

"I think we should talk," said the broom. "In private," he added sharply looking at the three women.

After they had moved from earshot, Mr Bristles addressed the others. "Listen, we have them where we want them."

"I 'ain't makin any deals wiv that woman…'ave you fergotten what that cow did to our boy! Wi'd be betrayin 'im," said Mrs Roly indignantly.

"That's not what I'm talking about!"

"Well spit it out then," said Mrs Pan. "What's yer plan?"

The broom gestured for them all to gather around, lowering his voice until it was barely audible. "Now listen to me…this is our chance to avenge the way that foul woman has treated Isaac. We say we'll help her in return for our freedom…"

"Where does the revenge part come in?" interrupted Mrs Pan irritably.

"We make the food look, smell and taste fantastic but we also add our own special ingredients that makes everybody feel sick to the stomach and exposes that woman for what she really is - a fraud! So what do you say? Are you with me?"

"What if they discover what we are doing before we are freed, and how can we be certain they will give us our freedom?" asked Sizzle Fizzle, the frying pan.

"It's a risk we have to take, but I believe a risk worth taking. Even if it is just for avenging poor Isaac for everything she put him through."

"Hear, hear!" said Mrs Roly.

"Firstly, we need to make the deal convincing otherwise they will be suspicious, secondly, we need to make two versions of everything so that if they check – which I am sure they will – they will not realise the affect the wedding feast will have on them and their guests."

"Do you really think we can get away with it?" asked Glinty.

"This is the chance we've been waiting for," urged Mr Bristles. "What say you all? Are you up for this?"

"Well, I'm in!" said Mrs Roly.

The others looked at each other, nodding.

"Yeah! Bring it on," said Glinty.

Chapter Twenty-Nine
PREPARATIONS FOR A WEDDING

Oro was putting the finishing touches to his wedding outfit when Glace entered.

"That ghastly man, Devin Fortuno, is here with his wife. I thought you had concluded all business with him?"

"I had!" snapped Oro, adjusting the elaborate wig he was wearing.

"Well, you'd better find out what he wants," she said tartly. "They're waiting in the Inner Sanctum."

Oro marched through the castle until he arrived in the hallway. Devin was busy examining the dragon's claw whilst his wife was helping herself to a rare perfume made from the essence of death.

"This really is quite delightful," she purred, squirting herself with it. "Such a dark and desperate aroma."

"Put it down!" barked Oro. "A hundred people were killed to create that!"

"Oh so touchy! Is that any way to greet your wedding guests?"

"My what!" blustered Oro.

"We could hardly let such a joyful occasion pass without celebrating it with you, especially as it was us who brought you together in the first place," said Devin languidly. "Not to mention that your dear wife-to-be invited us."

"She did what?!"

"Such a delightful lady, don't you think?" Opal said sarcastically to her husband.

"A real peach. I'm sure you will be most happy together," said Devin. "I could be your best man if you liked…"

"That won't be necessary."

"Now don't be such a sour puss," crooned Opal.

"Why are you really here?" said Oro scowling.

"Well aside from the wedding, we wanted to know when you intended to put our little plan into action," said Devin casually, sitting down on a nearby couch.

"Firstly it's my plan!" snapped Oro.

"As you wish, my friend," Devin drawled, combing his hair back with his fingers.

"And secondly, it's none of your damn business!"

"Ah, now you see, that's not exactly correct…after all, we have a vested interest - 30% of all the territories was what we agreed. I don't think it's unreasonable to ask that you share your plans with us. There must be some trust between us," he continued, twiddling his beard.

"Our deal has been finalised so why don't you go and crawl back under the stone that you came from! "

"So be it, but equally do not suppose that you can trick me! It is a well-known fact that your assassins have long and silent knives. I would be foolish to suppose that once you have taken control of Zartarbia you would keep your end of the bargain. So you will understand why I have taken the precautionary measure of detailing our meetings and placing them in flying envelopes addressed to the rest of our dear Syndicate associates – I just have

Dorian Gllittergold gets ready for her wedding

to say the word and they will wing their way to Tempest, Flores, Espectro and Fingimiento, along with the antidote…"

"Don't think to blackmail me, Fortuno!" said Oro, banging his fist on a table.

"Tut, tut, tut…Let's not get our knickers in a twist!" said Opal, sitting down next to her husband.

"We had to have insurance because, like you, I don't trust anybody either," said Devin pointedly.

"How dare you threaten me! I could crush you like an ant!" roared Oro, grabbing Devin by the collar and hauling him to his feet.

"And therein lies the problem," smiled Devin, pulling away his attacker's hand. "I don't want to be looking over my shoulder for the rest of my life. I'm simply giving you a word of advice – if you try to double-cross me, or have me eliminated, then the letters will be sent. So, now that little matter has been cleared up, how about a toast to the groom," Devin poured some champagne and offered a glass to Cazador.

Oro flung the contents of the glass over Devin's face. "You come to my home and think you can play me!"

Devin slowly wiped his face with the back of his sleeve. "I shall pretend that didn't happen. Clearly the stress of your wedding day has clouded your judgement. Perhaps you need some time to reflect on the basis of our alliance."

Oro glared at him but refrained from saying anything. Instead he snapped his fingers at a nearby butler. "Take these guests to their quarters and make sure they have everything that they need."

"Always the gracious host," said Opal waspishly.

"We'll just make ourselves at home then," grinned Devin.

"Don't push your luck, Fortuno!" growled Oro. "Just don't push your luck."

"Are you sure the girl is coming here?" whispered Opal as they made their way up to their suite of rooms.

"Oh yes, my crystal ball never lies," said Devin. "She's coming. We just have to find her – but we will have the locket before the night is out. She won't escape us this time!"

Meanwhile...

Dorian Glittergold was being primped and pampered by her two cousins. She sat in front of a huge mirror with Tootles on her lap, whilst Lady Dee and Lady Dah fussed over her. One removed rollers from her hair, whilst the other dusted her face with powder.

"You're going to look heavenly, my dear."

"Yes, a sight for sore eyes," Lady Dee caught Lady Dah's eyes as she said this, and they both stifled a giggle.

Lady Dah applied some blusher to Dorian's cheeks. "You can enjoy your special day now, safe in the knowledge..."

"...that there is nothing to worry about," finished Lady Dee as she sprayed hairspray over her cousin.

"I do feel much calmer now that I know the magic cutlery has agreed to do the wedding feast," said Dorian, admiring her reflection in the mirror.

"It is just about keeping the workers happy," agreed Lady Dee.

"By this evening you will be the new Mrs Cazador."

"You'll be running the household."

"And we'll be here to help you!"

There was a sharp knock on the door.

"My dear lady, may I come in?" called Oro Cazador.

"Goodness me, no!" shrieked the two sisters in unison. "Don't you know it's bad luck for the groom to see the bride before they are married!"

"I just wanted to check on Malveo's progress for this evening's banquet," said Oro.

"Oh, rest assured, my love, he's working away as we speak," replied Dorian.

"Good, I want everything to be perfect."

"It will be my love. Everything is going according to plan. I am sure you will be delighted with the results."

"Oh by the way, Devin Fortuno and Opal Luvie have arrived. I didn't know you had invited them."

"Well I thought it would be nice, especially as they are such good friends of yours. If it hadn't been for them, I might never have met you – just think of that!" she trilled cheerfully.

"Yes, just think of that!" muttered Oro darkly.

That evening, after the wedding ceremony had been performed, the feast was duly laid out. Silver platter after silver platter were bought out to the assembled party. The lids were lifted to reveal the most exquisite looking dishes. There were pigeons stuffed with almonds; quails in rose petal sauce; roulades of smoked salmon, avocado and crab; pork and apricot terrines. Carrots had been cut into the shape of flowers and leeks sliced to look like fountains. An enormous wedding cake was decorated with sugar-coated cherry blossoms.

All the guests' mouths watered furiously as the delicious aroma of the food filled the room. The smell was so intoxicating that their fingers itched to pick up the knives and forks but they did not dare until Oro had given the signal.

"Papa, will you excuse me for one moment," said Lily Rose.

"But we are just about to eat," said Oro looking at her in surprise.

"I have a special wedding surprise for you, I just wanted to go and get it."

"Get it later, my dear."

"Oh please Papa, it will only take a moment."

"Alright then. But hurry back as you wouldn't want to miss out on this fabulous feast."

Madame Glittergold smiled apprehensively at her new husband. "I hope this is to your satisfaction, my love."

"Your son has done us proud," he said, standing up and tapping his glass.

"I wish to propose a toast to my new wife, Dorian, and her son, Malveo, for organising this most wondrous of banquets. Now! Let us eat before the food gets cold!"

The guests needed no further prompting as they began to devour the sumptuous dishes. At first the food seemed to melt on their tongues, the delectable flavours flowing down their throats, then suddenly all the wedding guests started to feel nauseous. Soon they were all retching and vomiting. The room became a scene of chaos as they desperately tried to find bowls and plant pots to be sick in.

"What is this? You have poisoned the food!" roared Oro, throwing down his napkin.

"No! My darling husband! I don't know what has happened!" said a horrified Dorian, as she tried to quell the growing feeling of queasiness.

"You have deceived me!" Oro shouted at his trembling bride.

"My love, please! I'm so sorry. There's been some terrible mistake!" she gagged, before throwing up into her handbag.

"You're damn right there's been a terrible mistake!"

"Is it really so important? I mean the main thing is that we love each other…"

"Of course it's important, you sour-faced hag…why else do you think I married you?!" Oro tore off his long curly wig and threw it at her.

Dorian Glittergold went deathly white as her worst fears were realised.

"You tricked me! You have made a complete fool of me. Guards!

Take her to the dungeon…she can starve to death and the same goes for her son and cousins!"

"No, please!" shrieked Dorian.

Lady Dee and Lady Dah stared aghast before sliding out of their seats in a dead faint.

"Do you honestly think I would let you keep your life? Take them away!" bellowed Oro before he too was violently sick all over the table.

Only two guests remained untouched by the collective illness – Devin and Opal who quietly slipped away amidst the bedlam.

Chapter Thirty
THE DUNGEON OF SKELETONS

The sewer tunnels had been difficult to navigate but with Capitán Miguel guiding the fleet of ships they finally arrived safely at Segregaria. They had entered via a drain into the moat that surrounded Cazador's castle. They moored the boats and followed the rat through a small metal grid that led to the dungeons.

"Stay close to me," whispered Jet to Isabella and Isaac. "There will be soldiers everywhere."

They crept through the opening and one by one jumped down. The only slight problem came when three rats that were carrying Jangle, accidentally dropped the key on the floor which made a loud clang as he hit the stone.

"Hey be careful!" exclaimed Jangle.

"Sssshhh!" said Jet. "Nobody make a sound!"

Jet and Blaze scanned the corridor for guards, but there were none in sight.

"Good. I don't think anybody heard us. Now we need to ascertain exactly where Lujzka and Chloe are being held."

"I think da main dungeon is dis way. I go first to see," said Capitán Miguel scampering off.

"Is everybody clear on what we need to do when we find them?" asked Jet.

The assembled group nodded.

"Es clear," said Capitán Miguel. "You follow me."

"OK, let's go then," said Jet.

They set off down the corridor until they arrived at a large metal door.

"Right, let's resize. Stand well apart from each other," said Jet brusquely, quickly swallowing a phial of liquid similar to the one Lujzka had given Isabella and Isaac. The others did the same. Jet picked up Jangle and after several attempts, the key unlocked the door.

There was barely any light inside the dungeon but Isabella could just about make out three crouched figures surrounded by numerous skeletons.

"Lujzka? Is that you?" Isabella whispered.

The three figures looked up, their mouths gagged with dirty rags, their hands and feet tied tightly with rope.

"Agent Lujzka, Agent Chloe, good to see you again!" said Jet, rushing over to untie them. "Are you alright?"

Lujzka nodded weakly as Jet removed the restraint from her mouth.

"Thank God, I thought I was going to rot in here forever," she said, gasping for breath.

"Hey, do you really think Detective Valise would allow that to happen? We couldn't lose our best agent," Jet grinned.

Lujzka looked at Isaac, puzzled.

"It's Isaac," began Isabella, seeing her friend's confusion. "I'll explain later."

Lujzka smiled and nodded, feeling too sore and exhausted to react further.

Jet and Blaze quickly freed Chloe, who was barely conscious.

"I'm going to have to carry her," said Blaze. "She's too frail to walk by herself."

"Who's this guy?" said Jet, pointing at the third figure.

"It's Spike Pennypinch, the manager of the hotel," said Lujzka.

"What's he doing here?"

"Betrug Espion was interrogating him about his boss, Dorian Glittergold. He thought he was using a truth potion on him, but Chloe had managed to switch it for a forgetfulness potion before she was captured, so he didn't get anything out of him. By the time Espion realised, it was too late," said Lujzka, struggling to her feet.

"So he knows nothing?" said Jet.

"No, not at the moment but it's only a matter of time. I heard the guards talking earlier on that Cazador and Glittergold were to be married today. Malveo was to prepare the wedding banquet, so they will know he's not the real chef. We have to get out of here before he realises."

"So what do we do about him?" said Jet, gesturing to Spike.

"Well we can't leave him to die here," said Lujzka.

"What about what he's done to Isaac? All the abuse?" said Isabella.

"Whatever he's done to me, he doesn't deserve to be left here. I hate him for the way he treated me but I wouldn't wish a death like this on anybody," said Isaac quietly, "If I let him die here then I am as bad as him."

"I agree. He'll pay for his crimes but not like this," replied Lujzka, as Jet walked over to Spike and undid his bonds.

"Thank you," said Spike, looking bewildered. "Who are all these people?"

"Never you mind!" said Jet sharply. "You'd better keep up because we won't be coming back for you!"

In the distance footsteps could be heard approaching in their direction.

"We need to get out of here, right now!" said Jet. "Come on everybody! We need to get out!"

Blaze lifted Chloe across his shoulders and quickly they all ran back towards the grid opening, but they were too late. Their escape route was blocked. Coming towards them were several guards dragging three screaming women and a boy – Madame Glittergold, her two cousins and her son Malveo.

"This way!" whispered Lujzka. "We've got no choice!"

"How are we going to get out?" said Isabella.

"We'll find a way," said Blaze, as they charged down another corridor, away from the soldiers. They rounded another corner and as they did, they collided with two people running in the opposite direction. It was difficult to tell who was more shocked.

"Who are you?" said Lily Rose, looking nervously at them. "You look familiar."

"I'm an FADF agent, Miss Cazador," said Lujzka. "You might have seen me at the Hotel Gastronomic. We need to find a way out of here or your father will murder us. Will you help us?"

"An FADF agent?"

"Yes."

"Then you are an enemy of my father," she said. "You want to kill him!"

"No. You father's solution to those that oppose him might be death but we believe in justice…and I think you do as well."

Lily looked at Orlando uncertainly, who nodded.

"I'll help you but only if you can help us. We're in love, we're running away. Once my father realises he will not rest until he has found us. Can the FADF protect us?"

"Yes. We can protect you, but time is running out!" said Jet.

"Follow me," said Lily. "There is a secret passageway to the gardens. It comes out by the far side of the moat."

In the background there was a sudden uproar as the guards discovered the unlocked dungeon and raised the alarm.

It seemed like ages before they emerged outside by the bottom of the tall walls that protected the castle. Capitán Miguel hopped out of Lujzka's pocket and on to her shoulder. He took out a telescope and trained it to where they had moored the ships.

"Si, dey still dere but we must be muy rapido," he said excitedly.

They had almost reached the boats when Oro Cazador stepped out from the shadow of a tree, followed by Espion and Glace.

The group stopped dead in their tracks as an army of soldiers surrounded them, guns loaded and pointed at them. All appeared hopelessly lost.

"It would appear we have some gatecrashers," said Oro coldly, walking over to them.

He took his daughter's face in his hands. "Lily, I am most disappointed in you. You were going to leave me weren't you? Why would you do this to me? I love you."

Lily gulped with fear, her voice quivering, "You don't love me, you just want to control me…"

He squeezed her jaw. "Be quiet! Like mother, like daughter. What were you thinking?"

"Papa, please!"

"Leave her alone!" shouted Orlando, lunging towards him.

Gunfire riddled the night and Orlando fell to the ground.

"No!" screamed Lily breaking away from her father. She ran to her lover, holding him tightly, his blood seeping all over her clothes.

"He's still breathing! Somebody help me!"

Lujzka and Jet started to move towards the tragic couple.

"Stay where you are!" roared Oro pulling out a dagger. "Your time will come soon enough. And as for you Lily, I command you to move out of the way – NOW!"

Lily clung to Orlando, sobbing, "No, I won't! What have you done? You're nothing more than a murderer…I hate you!"

"I said get out of the way!" he said advancing on her.

"NO! You will have to kill me first!"

Oro looked at her. "Is that what you really want?" he whispered, his face ashen. "After all the love I have bestowed on you?"

"I want my freedom," Lily sobbed. Oro stared for a moment longer, then turned away, raising a hand.

A single shot was fired and Lily fell to the ground.

Chapter Thirty-One
THE DEATH OF TWO LOVERS

Everybody stood in stunned silence. The air turned icy cold and snow began to swirl down on them. All that could be heard was wind whistling in their ears. Oro seemed to turn in slow motion, his jaw slack as he stared in surprise, shock and horror at his daughter's lifeless body, slumped over the body of her lover. His bulky frame heaved with sorrow and for a moment he looked quite helpless. "What have I done?"

Jet stepped forward to say something, but Oro turned on him suddenly. "I blame you. I blame you all!" he roared angrily, "You should never have come here!"

Then he turned to his guards. "Kill them, kill them all!"

"Run!" Lujzka shouted to Isabella and Isaac as the guards started to reload their guns. "We'll hold them off the best we can!"

"Quickly, everybody! Put on your protector activations!" yelled Jet, pulling a small cord on his suit which immediately produced a transparent sphere of armour around his body. Jet, Blaze and Lujzka sprung into action, back flipping over the guards. They moved so fast, with a speed that defied belief. The protective armour deflected the bullets. The rats fought bravely too, biting the legs of the soldiers and poking them with their tiny swords which in truth did nothing but cause mild irritation. Capitán Miguel ran with the children, leading them back inside the secret passage.

"Where are we going?" said Isaac.

"I don't know amigo, but I find a way out for us," said the rat breathlessly.

Behind them they could hear the battle raging.

"I hope they're going to be alright. There were so many guards," said Isabella.

"Dey trained FADF agents, dey know Quing Chaitsu! Don't worry, chica! Da FADF will send reinforcements!"

"Someone's in a hurry," said Devin sneaking up behind them. "So we meet at last Miss Isabella - I've been waiting a long time for this and so good of you to have brought me the Locket of Fire and Water."

Isabella gasped with shock and before she could escape, Opal Luvie grabbed her arms, pinning them behind her.

"Not so fast my pretty, we have plans for you!" she said, holding her tight.

"You no touch the children. I guard dem with my life, you let her go!" shouted Capitán Miguel, pointing his sword at them.

"Well, what do we have here?" smirked Devin, picking the rodent up by his tail.

"I smell a rat," Opal Luvie sniggered with laughter.

Capitán Miguel twisted and turned, trying to bite Devin.

"And you must be the secret chef - two for the price of one. Today just keeps getting better, doesn't it beloved?" he said smiling at his wife.

"You let dem go!"

"Shut up, you furry little pest!" snapped Fortuno, hurling Capitán Miguel against the wall. "Let's get out of here before that old fool Cazador realises."

They dragged the struggling children outside again, over to where a hot air balloon was waiting with a stretch limousine attached to it.

"Leaving so soon!" said Jet Black advancing on them, two swords drawn.

In the distance they could see reinforcement FADF agents rolling out of the sky, unwinding down on long pieces of fabric.

"The game's up, Fortuno!"

"I don't think so. I hold all the cards as you can see," he sneered pulling the two children in front of him. "You wouldn't want them to get hurt now would you?"

"I won't let you leave with them."

"From where I'm standing you have no choice. Now stay back, or I shall kill them. Do you really want to have their blood on your hands?"

Devin started to edge backwards towards the balloon and it was at that moment that hundreds of birds descended on him and his wife, pecking at his face and hands until he was forced to let go of the children. They ran through the flurry of feathers to Jet Black.

"Ah, get off!" Fortuno screamed, his arms flaying as he tried to swipe them away.

"Quickly my love, we must get to safety before we are pecked to pieces!" shrieked Opal, stumbling towards the limousine and throwing herself inside.

"I'm not leaving without the locket!" he shouted, trying to lunge at Isabella but the birds beat him back, scratching at his eyes with their claws until he too was forced to jump into the waiting car. And with that they were gone, the car and balloon whooshed into the sky with the speed of a rocket.

"Are you two alright?" said Jet, putting an arm around each of them. "You were really brave."

The children nodded, hugging him tightly.

"Ah dere you are!" exclaimed Capitán Miguel as he scampered over to them, "I worried dat dey harm you."

"We're fine," said Isabella. "What about you?"

"My hat is a bit battered but eh, no matter! I have der heart of a lion. Noting scare me!" shrugged the rat.

"Eh what is dat?" he said as his beady eyes caught sight of something glinting by a rock. He scurried over, sniffing the object. Jet followed him, picking it up. "I don't believe it! It's The Box of Reversals! Fortuno must have dropped it in all the confusion."

"Finders' keepers, amigo," said the rat, trying to take it back.

"Sorry Capitán, but this will need to be taken to Securical for further investigation. This is a most powerful box. It contains magic strong enough to change history if combined with the other sacred objects. I'm sure you will be rewarded with a medal for your discovery though. Well done, you have done Zartarbia a great service."

"A medal you say? Well, dat better than nothing I guess," he said, picturing himself sporting a shiny medal for his bravery.

By now the FADF agents outnumbered Cazador's guards by about two to one and though the fighting continued for a short while longer, it was clear that they would have to surrender. One by one, the soldiers were handcuffed and taken away until only Cazador and Glace remained. Jet and Blaze couldn't find Betrug, who had slipped away in disguise as soon as he saw that the battle was lost.

They stood surrounded by agents, their hands in the air. Lujzka was reading them their rights, "I am arresting you on the charges of high treason against Zartarbia in accordance with FADF law and of murder in the first degree. How many counts has yet to be established but rest assured, Mr Cazador, we will take Segregaria apart brick by brick until we have discovered the truth. You will now be taken to Encasaration where you will remain until a date for your trial has been set."

"How could you have let this happen?" hissed Glace to her brother. "You fool!"

"Take them away!" said Lujzka, turning her back on them.

"I want to see my daughter before I go," said Oro quietly, "to say goodbye."

Lujzka hesitated and with a quick look at Jet, she then nodded.

She escorted him to Lily's body that still lay across her lover's, their blood saturating the snow around them.

"I loved you so much," he said, bending down to touch his daughter's frozen cheek.

"Then how could you instruct your guards to kill her?" said Lujzka coldly.

Oro looked up, tears coursing down his face. "I didn't…I didn't mean to… I don't know what happened. I was so angry. My little girl, my only child wanted to leave me. How could I allow that to happen?"

"Except Lily wasn't your little girl anymore, she was a grown woman. She had her whole life in front of her and you took it away!" said Lujzka in disgust. "Get him out of my sight!"

"Wait a moment!" said Jet pulling The Box of Reversals out of his jacket. "There might just be a way to bring them back to life. Isabella, are you able to take off your locket? It's just that if we place it within the box, there might just be a chance that we can undo their deaths."

She glanced anxiously at Jet and Lujzka, before putting The Locket of Fire and Water into the box. Isabella placed the box on top of Lily and Orlando's bodies and they waited silently, snowflakes softly falling. They waited, and waited – but nothing happened.

"Well it was worth trying," said Jet finally. "We had best take the bodies for burial."

"No, wait a moment more!" pleaded Isabella.

"It's no good. At least they're together now," he said sadly.

"Hang on!" said Lujzka suddenly, remembering something she had once read. "What if it only works by the hand of the person who is responsible for their death? Maybe he is the only one who can give back life?" she said, turning and looking at Cazador.

"No," he said shaking his head. "I would prefer her to sleep in peace."

"How can she? She didn't die in peace!" said Lujzka harshly, thrusting the box into his shackled hands. "If you really love your daughter then do this one thing for her. If you truly love your daughter then prove it! It's your fault they're dead. The least you can do is try!"

Oro looked at the box and then at his daughter, slowly placing it on her.

"I'm doing this for her," he said to no-one in particular, "not to save my own skin."

Immediately a glow emitted from the box, spreading across the young lovers. The blood disappeared from the snow little by little and the wounds they had suffered closed over. Colour returned to their faces and they drew breath into their lungs. The assembled group clapped their hands in delight.

"It worked, they're alive!" shrieked Isabella embracing Lujzka.

Lily Rose gradually sat up shivering. "It's so cold. What has happened?"

Orlando stirred beside her. "My love, you're alive!"

Lily stood up awkwardly and embraced her lover, suddenly she noticed her father and a look of terror momentarily crossed her face. "It's alright. He can't harm you now," said Lujzka, placing a reassuring hand on her elbow. "Once darkness is overcome, then only light can prevail. You're free now."

Lily nodded kissing Orlando.

"I'm sorry, Lily," said Oro, fixing his glass eye on her, "really I am."

"I'm sorry too."

Father and daughter looked at each other one last time, neither saying a word, before he was led away, a broken man.

Chapter Thirty-Two
ISABELLA RECOUNTS HER ADVENTURES
TO AUNTY CIS

"So what happened after that?" asked Aunty Cis, nibbling her twentieth biscuit. "Come on, you can't leave me in suspense!"

Isabella smiled, sipping a glass of lemonade. "Well, needless to say Oro and Glace were placed in Encasaration - which is a top security prison. They were found guilty and Detective Valise says they'll never be let out. They found more than two hundred skeletons bricked into the walls of his castle. How can anybody be so cruel?"

"Unfortunately evil lurks in some people's hearts. He sounds a real Blue Beard!" said Aunty Cis shaking her head. "What happened to the others?"

"Well, Lily Rose and Orlando got married and adopted Isaac, and they moved back to the hotel with the magic cutlery. They're going to use the profits to subsidise a local orphanage."

"An admirable sentiment. I like a happy ending. It makes a refreshing change from all the doom and gloom those news presenters have to report."

"Well it wasn't happy for everybody. Madame Glittergold, Malveo and Spike were all sentenced to a lifetime of hard labour.

The FADF have ensured that they have to spend the rest of their days building shelters and schools for the underprivileged in Sumptitious. Lady Dee and Lady Dah turned state witnesses against their cousin to save their own skins. Still they weren't let off the hook completely, they were forced to attend a Rehabilitation Group for the Selfish and Stupid."

"I'd have given them all detention for the rest of their lives!" said Aunty Cis crossly. "I always say that what goes around, comes around."

"Anyway, they can never hurt Isaac again. He's happy now."

"And what of that Fortuno chap?" said Aunty Cis taking yet another biscuit.

"We don't know. The FADF are still trying to track him down," shrugged Isabella.

"He sounds a slippery character," said Aunty Cis peering over the top of her glasses.

"He is," nodded Isabella, "and his wife is just as bad!"

"And all of these adventures before teatime? Well I never!"

"So did you miss me?"

"I always miss you, though you were only gone an hour or so… I tell you what, your mother has been driving me mad. This medicine and that medicine – I know she means well, but she makes me feel as if I'm an invalid. I might be old, but I'm not totally decrepit yet!" said Aunty Cis indignantly.

"You won't mention any of this to mama, will you? You have to promise me…"

Aunty Cis looked at her mischievously. "Well I don't know! Don't worry I won't say anything."

Isabella paused. "She always seems so angry with me."

Aunty Cis shook her head, "She loves you, she doesn't know how to show it sometimes. You're growing up so fast. She wants

Orlando, Lily Rose and Isaac

you to stay her little girl that's all – like Lily Rose. Parents don't always know how to adjust."

"Why are we always fighting then?"

"It was the same when I was a child, you just have to find your own way but remember you only have one mother! And you mustn't forget that my being ill has put your mother under a lot of stress and extra work recently," Aunty Cis leant forward, "It would be very big of you if you made the first move. It will probably bring you closer together than ever before."

Isabella nodded, knowing by the warm glow that spread through her heart that Aunty Cis was right.

"So tell me about that key again…" said Aunty Cis, wiping some crumbs from her tweed skirt.

"Jangle?"

"Yes, Jangle - sounds like a Christmas chorus to me."

Isabella chuckled. "Don't let him hear you say that! Well, after I left the attic…"

Epilogue
THE RESIDENCE OF PROFESSOR CHARLES MORTENSEN, KNIGHTBRIDGE, LONDON.

150 YEARS AGO.

Mrs Beatrice Mortensen was busy fiddling with the flower arrangements when the doorbell sounded. 'Who can be calling at this hour?' she thought, thinking it was a rather inappropriate time for anybody to visit. The grandfather clock in the hallway showed 11.30pm and normally she was in bed by this point. The staff had retired for the evening and she wasn't accustomed to greeting visitors in person.

She glanced at her husband's study, wondering whether she should ask him to go and see who might bother them at such an unsociable hour. The doorbell rang again, this time more insistently.

'Well really!' she thought. 'This is most odd. I suppose it must be important.'

The bell was still jangling with a most rapid determination when she reluctantly opened the door. A hooded figure stood there, dripping with water.

"Do you know what time it is?" she said, masking her apprehension.

The old man pulled back his hood, "I am sorry to trouble you. I must speak to the master of the house urgently – I must speak with Professor Mortensen!"

She gasped when she saw who it was. "I thought I told you last time, your sort are not welcome here!" She moved to shut the door in his face.

"I understand you may not welcome me personally, but I believe your good husband will be most interested in what I have to tell him. I don't mean to alarm you, but it really is of the utmost urgency. I beg you let me in – there are people following me!" he said pushing his way in and slamming the door behind him.

"Charles! Charles! There is an intruder. He's forced his way in!" shrieked his wife backing away and grabbing the nearest weapon to hand, which happened to be an umbrella.

"What the hell is going on!" shouted Professor Mortensen, storming into the hallway. He stopped dead in his tracks when he saw the Merchant, and his attitude changed. "I was wondering when I would see you again. Beatrice, it's fine. This gentleman is an acquaintance of mine."

"But my dear, this was the unsavoury character I told you about – you know the one that turned up here unannounced the night of your accident," she whispered, giving him a knowing look. "He has not even offered a calling card, he just barged in... the rudeness! Are you seriously suggesting that he is a colleague of yours!"

Charles Mortensen took his wife gently by the elbow and guided her towards the stairs. "My dear, he has been on a weary journey and I am sure he cannot be bothered with social etiquette at this late hour. I shall look after him if you wish to retire. I shall see you later," he said firmly.

"If you are sure, my dear..."

"I'm sure," he said, kissing her chastely on her cheek.

The Merchant took off his cloak and hung it carefully on the coat stand.

"What the hell happened that night! I thought you had been abducted or worse! Come through to the study. We need to talk as I've made some interesting discoveries where those documents are concerned."

The Merchant followed him, seating himself down without being invited. He pulled off a pair of soaking wet leather boots and proceeded to take off the foulest smelling socks you could ever imagine.

"Ah, that's better," he said. "You have truly abominable weather at the moment. The camels are most unsettled by it. I had to leave them with a cousin of mine in Whitechapel. They ren't happy, of course, but at least they are sheltered. So e you solved the puzzle yet?"

"You have a nerve Sir! You have created chaos in my life, turn up at this late hour demanding answers! Why did you me that locket and the parchments?"

'You know why, but I did suspect you would have problems finding the missing pieces...."

'What are you expecting me to find?" snapped Professor rtensen.

'Well, you're one step closer to knowing," said the Merchant bing his stubbly chin.

'That is no answer. Damn you, Sir! Why do you always e to talk in riddles?"

he old man simply smiled and put his feet next to the fire. thing like a bit of warmth through the old bones."

You either know the answer, or you don't!" said Mortensen circling around him.

"Look, I said before...I'm an old man. I don't have the time or energy for such exertions - I'm exhausted by life. You on the other hand have an inquisitive mind, you challenge general perceptions. I know you value your social standing - that I can comprehend - but this is something different. You know it and I know it."

"You know nothing about me!" said Mortensen crossly.

"That is where you are wrong, I know a lot about you; it's why I selected you Professor, but you know I am not here to exchange pleasantries," replied the old man evenly.

"Then why the hell are you here?"

"Teufel Alma."

"Who?"

"Teufel Alma is the man who accosted me in The Lion and Eagle Tavern. He is a criminal mastermind and a dedicated disciple of black magic. He knows about Zartarbia and wants to make it his own."

"What are you talking about? How can he know?" said the Professor.

The Merchant rubbed his face wearily. "I have something to confess, I'm afraid. Before I realised the great importance of the locket, I took it to various experts to have it valued - in case I decided to sell it, you understand. Alma was one of those "experts". He offered to buy it on the spot but there was something about him that terrified me. When I looked into his eyes there was pure unadulterated evil. I knew I wouldn't have got away with my life, so I told him about the parchments, that they had the same markings. I said I would fetch them immediately and, with that, I went into hiding. I have no idea how he found me in the tavern that evening but he has spies everywhere. He's had his people watching your house for weeks now. You must be most careful my friend, he is a murderer most foul."

"If my memory serves me correctly, it was he who called you a murderer that evening!"

"That's a lie! I'm here to help."

"How? By putting me and my family in danger?!"

"Tell me what you have so far discovered?"

"I'm not telling you anything until you tell me what the hell you have got me in to!" snapped Mortensen.

"Calm down! Yes, Teufel Alma is after you, but he will wait until you have cracked the code. It gives us time though you need to get your family to safety immediately. It is why I came back. Look I know you're angry..."

"Angry? Angry! I think you should get out of my house. You've caused enough trouble...and take these damn things with you!" he said thrusting the locket and documents into the old man's hands.

"I can't take back what doesn't belong to me," he said placing them on the table. "And that is the other reason for my visit... you see they have changed ownership, the power has been transferred."

"What! To whom? Me?"

The Merchant shook his head. "No, somebody that is completely pure, like Zartarbia itself."

"Nobody else has seen the parchments," said the Professor, combing his hair with his fingers.

"I don't think that is exactly true. What about The Locket of Fire and Water? Somebody else has touched it?"

"No...wait a minute my wife, she picked it up a few days ago."

"No, it's not her. You have a daughter I believe," said the Merchant slowly.

"Auriel? How do you know that?"

"It doesn't matter, but I believe she has touched the necklace…"

"Impossible. She couldn't have. She isn't permitted into my study and besides I keep it under lock and key," said Mortensen frowning.

"That may well be, but a child has handled this locket and I think it's your daughter. If she has, then she controls it now. She is the key and the moment Teufel Alma realises this, well, the consequences could be devastating!"

"Oh my God!"

"Is she asleep?"

"Yes, I think so…"

"Then I urge you, go and wake her, wake your wife too – we must take them somewhere safe, right now!"

Professor Mortensen jumped to his feet and bounded up the stairs, his heart pounding. The Merchant heard him cry out. "Oh my God! They're gone! They're both gone!"

"So it is too late, he has got them," the Merchant said under his breath shaking his head. "The devil is upon us."

Notes to the Reader

WELCOME TO THE STRANGE WORLD OF ZARTARBIA

To understand Zartarbia, one must first imagine a jigsaw puzzle that constantly moves, each piece interlinking with another, shifting border to border. The various territories change shape and size (which can be a cause of great tension between those who live there). Sometimes areas of land sink underground, sometimes islands resurface through the seas.

(You will see I have attempted to draw a map for you but as I have already mentioned the lands transform and evolve without reason, so it is just to give you an idea of how it might look and of course, it is not drawn to scale – that would be impossible!)

As with most countries that we are familiar with, there must be dark and light, elements of bad and good - and Zartarbia is no exception.

THE HISTORY OF ZARTARBIA

In the beginning, Zartarbia was a paradise where everybody lived harmoniously. It was created by a High Priest of Arequipa in ancient Peru who had become sickened by the bloodthirsty influence of an evil Aztec King who ruled the lands. Along with this perfect world, he created four key elements to protect the innocence of Zartarbia. Unfortunately he was deceived by his assistant, who betrayed the High Priest to the King in return for great riches. Once the High Priest discovered what had happened, he buried his treacherous assistant alive, without realising he had stolen documents and the Locket of Fire and Water to give to the Aztec King as proof.

As the king and his army approached, the High Priest told his family and fellow worshipers to escape to Zartarbia. They begged him to come with them, but he could not, as somebody had to seal the gateway permanently to ensure Zartarbia's safety. And for many centuries it was indeed a promised land - there were no struggles for power, no wars and crime was unheard of. It was an ancient world seeped in magic and innocence.

Centuries later, an explorer discovered the skeleton of the untrustworthy assistant along with the items that were accidentally buried with him. The explorer (not realising the great power of the objects) exchanged them with an old merchant; one of the items was the necklace that held a pathway into this untouched world. Realising the power of his discovery and he took the locket to the renowned Professor Mortensen (famous for his work on ancient civilisations) but dark forces were already aware of the existence of Zartarbia and wanted to access it for themselves. This is where the struggle between good and evil began.

Seven Deadly Sins were unleashed upon the unsuspecting inhabitants of Zartarbia. It was an experiment conducted by a criminal mastermind Teufel Alma, who wanted to cultivate a monstrous army to take over the earth and as you will discover in the following books of this series, he almost succeeded......

The Seven Souls of Combatine were created to fight for good. In Zartarbia's recent past there was a great battle, after which things changed forever. This is a complex history and like any story, it takes a while to tell but we enter the story at the point when, many years later, ten year old Isabella Zophie discovers The Locket of Fire and Water in her great aunt's attic.

THE SYNDICATE OF SEVEN DEADLY SINS

The Syndicate was a direct result of the Seven Deadly Sins invading Zartarbia. They controlled all that was dark, drawing on the weakness and fear in people. There were seven leaders of The Syndicate all powerful and totally ruthless. Nobody trusted anybody else. That was the nature of the power they possessed - the more they had, the more they craved…whatever the cost. The members of The Syndicate, together with the sins they are descended from, are as follows:

Mistress Sectica (SIN: PRIDE)

She once owned the lands of Narcissimal and Tivany, enforcing her rule with an army of Gliders which were zombie-like creatures that were once children controlled by Sectica. Her vanity killed her in the first book, Isabella Zophie and the Cirque de Magique, for those of you that have not read it.

Oro Cazador (SIN: GLUTTONY)

He rules the lands of Glutonious and Segregaria. A self-indulgent man obsessed with acquiring rare and beautiful objects. He is used to getting his way at all costs and is one of the most forceful members of The Syndicate.

Tempest Pestilencia (SIN: ENVY)

He rules the Seas of Uncertainty. Tempest is a pirate that roams his watery kingdom, priding himself on his brutal success in plundering and intimidating all who get in his way.

Flores Abunda (SIN: LUST)

She reigns over The Forests of Longing. Flores is a beautiful but dangerous creature, who can break a man's heart and drive him to the depths of despair with a single look. Nobody is immune to her deadly charms except the other Syndicate members.

Espectro Underwelt (SIN:WRATH)
He controls the dark lands of Furioso and Petrifie, where sunlight never shines and the only lights are neon. He is the darkest of all the characters and all who meet him fear him. His body is tattooed with the souls of the undead.

Fingimiento (SIN: GREED)
He rules the lands of Avaricen and Excessiton with his armies of Transcenders which are chameleon-type creatures that can change shape and are often used as spies.

He is the most mysterious of The Syndicate members, who always wears masks so nobody knows what he really looks like.

Devin Fortuno (SIN: SLOTH)
He lives in the city of Lethargical with his equally lazy but very ambitious wife, Opal Luvie, where they spend their time in the pursuit of pleasure. A self-styled soothsayer who is a devious and sly character.

THE FEDERATION AGAINST DARK FORCES
(The FADF)
However, all is not dark, because born out of fear is also hope. The other half of Zartarbia was very much dedicated to it's original existence of peaceful living, where people rebelled against the tyranny of The Syndicate. They governed themselves democratically under the protection of the **FADF** (Federation Against Dark Forces) who, as you will discover, were more than capable opponents in this battle against evil. Detective Frederick

Valise heads this organisation and is a highly intelligent, if not rather eccentric, character. Lujzka and Jet Black are his two top FADF agents.

THE ZARTARBIAN TERRITORIES

The Free States (protected by the FADF):
Securical
Where the headquarters of the Federation Against Dark Forces are based. It is a high-tech city of glass contained in several enormous protective bubbles, and is the safest territory in Zartarbia.

The Island of Parisio
A stunning paradise where people live from the land, living simply.

The Moon Mountains
A quiet and tranquil place where its inhabitants create special night time stars, which they send out to watch over children as they sleep - like guardian angels.

Electrodia
Inhabited by Electrodians, a race of people that can generate energy and power from within themselves. All their clothes are made from light bulbs, their nails, teeth and even eyelashes.

Topsy Turney
Inhabited by the Bonker Lonkers, a crazy group of creatures who go through life doing everything back to front and inside out. Physically they are very tall, thin and extremely bendy like rubber.

Suerte

Mainly characterised by the fact that all its residents have incredibly good luck.

The Sacred Soul Mountains

This cold mountain range is very sparsely populated, with just one or two hermits living in caves. Legend has it that the Seven Souls of Combatine (if they still exist) are trapped somewhere in this land.

The City of Bon-Bons

A place of fun which is mostly run by orphaned children who all look after one another. Their houses are made from biscuits, cake and sweets.

Drimbledon

An ordinary place full of peaceful people who go about their daily business in a fairly mundane sort of way. Nothing much exciting ever happens here.

The Island of Encasaration

This island is basically a huge jail where all the most dangerous villains captured by the FADF are sent. The entire island is surrounded by an extremely sophisticated security system, making escape impossible.

Narcissimal & Tivany

These two territories were once ruled by Mistress Sectica, but after her death were placed under FADF protection.

THE OPPRESSED STATES:
Forcibly ruled by The Syndicate

Glutonious & Segregaria

Lands of excess, for some; the divide between the rich and the poor is huge. These areas are under tight security, and every occupant is forced to have a microchip implanted into them; they have to be scanned in and out everywhere they go. Oro Cazador controls these lands.

The Seas of Uncertainty

Governed by Tempest Pestilencia and his army of pirates, sea monsters and sirens. These waters are extremely dangerous and volatile, prone to storms.

The Forests of Longing

Ruled by Flores Abunda, where she lives in an ornate temple. These forests are lush and overgrown, full of weird and dangerous creatures. Her people are called the Desirals and are a very manipulative race.

Avaricen & Excessiton

Governed by Fingimiento who has various gigantic palaces, castles and mansions. These lands are most occupied by the Sufferans (a down-trodden race of people) and they are kept suppressed by the Transcenders (changelings who act as spies, bounty hunters etc)

Furioso & Petrifie

These underground worlds are the most dangerous of all the Zartarbian territories. They are ruled by Espectro Underwelt; both lands are neon graveyards for the undead.

Lethargical & Sumptitious

Owned by Devin Fortuno and his wife, Opal Luvie, who live in an opulent pleasure palace. As you will know from reading Book 2, Fortuno exchanges Sumptitious with Cazador.

THE NOMANSLANDS
(neither controlled nor protected):
Threadborton

A den of iniquity where the buildings move in and out as if they are breathing.

Froidon

A cold and unfriendly place inhabited by the Froidons, a fierce though loyal tribe of hunters.

THE BLEAK-LANDS
(Uninhabited areas)

The Distant Isles of Banishment

A series of small islands all of which have very hostile environments.

The Vortex Seas

A large and deadly area of water where vortexes spin up from the sea from nowhere, sucking any unfortunate victims to their deaths.

The Seas of Death

Underneath these treacherous waters lie ghostly skeletons constantly on the look out for new victims.

Bone Dessert

An arid wasteland of sand and stones. No plants grow here, and the only life forms that are capable of surviving in this climate are monstrous serpents.

Archtico

The temperature is so freezing in this land that a person would die in seconds.

So that gives you a brief idea of the history and geography of Zartarbia but you must understand that the stories are complex – I just hope you enjoy reading them as much as I have enjoyed writing them!

Let me know what you think, by e-mailing info@zartarbia.com or for further information, competitions and downloads visit our website at www.zartarbia.com

Best wishes
Ana Fischel
(Author and Illustrator of The Zartarbia Tales)

Tempest
Pestilencia

A skull and cross bones are on the horizon announcing the arrival of Book 3 arriving from a long journey in Spring 2006!

THE ZARTARBIA TALES
BOOK 3

Isabella Zophie and the Piraten

Written and Illustrated
by Ana Fischel

Submerge yourself in this third thrilling Zartarbian instalment - a swash-buckling adventure from the high seas and depths of the ocean!

Tempest Pestilencia (based on the Sin of Envy) is a brutal pirate who roams the deadly Seas of Uncertainty, surrounding himself with fierce monsters and sultry sirens. When he and Espectro Underwelt hatch a plot to unleash the terrifying Demonicals into Zartarbia, it is up to the FADF to stop them - assisted by Isabella Zophie. But there seems to be a spy in their midst...Is Devin Fortuno is up to his old tricks again?

And what of the beautiful Celestia, Espectro's wife, who is bound to a dark and dreadful secret? Before long the two Syndicate allies are pitted against one another – both determined to take what they want regardless of the consequences.

Will Isabella be able to prevent the tidal wave of their diabolical plans destroying the history of Zartarbia?

In the meantime, enter our competition:

CREATE YOUR OWN CHARACTER !!!!

We are inviting children to come up with their own Zartarbian characters - both visual drawings as well as a written description, perhaps even a short story line. You can use any medium you like (paints, pencils, collage etc) but your piece of artwork MUST be original and fit onto a piece of A4 paper.

Submissions can be either independently from individuals or via your school.
This can be run as an inter-school knock-out competition between schools in your local area* and the first, second and third place prize-winners will also receive a FREE copy of Book 2 to go into their school library.

FIRST PRIZE
The first place prize-winner will receive the following fantastic prizes:

YOUR character included in the third book of The Zartarbia Tales series:
Isabella Zophie & the Piraten
PLUS Ana Fischel will illustrate her interpretation of the character you have created for inclusion in Book 3 alongside your illustration
PLUS the winner will receive the signed, original piece of Ana Fischel's artwork of your character
PLUS a signed copy of Book 3 personalised to you – and a copy personalised to your school (if you entered via the inter-school knock-out competition)

SECOND AND THIRD PLACE
PRIZE-WINNERS

YOUR character illustration included at the back of Book 3, together with text describing your character
PLUS a signed copy of Book 3 personalised to you – and a copy personalised to your school (if you entered via the inter-school knock-out competition)

20 OF THE BEST ENTRIES

PLUS a signed copy of Book 3 for you and a copy for your school (if you entered via the inter-school knock-out competition)

Competition Rules and Guidelines:

- The competition is open to children up to and including the age of 16 years.
- Entries must be submitted via your parent or guardian – but please remember to mark which school you attend as there is going to be a regional 'knock-out' competition.
- No entries can be returned.
- All entries must be originals and on A4 paper.
- Closing date is 31st December, 2005.
- Judge's decision is final.
- No relatives of Pen Press, D'Image, Web Studio or Zartarbia Ltd may enter.

A full list of rules can be found on www.zartarbia.com

If you are not based in England, please submit your entries directly to Zartarbia Ltd, Spain (see overleaf) for judging independently of the inter-school 'knock-out' competition.

ENTRY FORM

CHILD'S NAME: ....

AGE: .... DATE OF BIRTH: ....

SCHOOL YEAR:.. ....

PARENT'S NAME: ....

PARENT/GUARDIAN SIGNATURE...

ADDRESS:
....

....

CONTACT EMAIL:..

CONTACT PHONE NUMBER:
....

SCHOOL NAME:
....

SCHOOL ADDRESS:..

....

....

....

YOUR DESCRIPTION OF THE CHARACTER
YOU HAVE CREATED:

I confirm that I am 16 years or under: ☐ YES ☐ NO

I confirm that the submitted artwork is ☐ YES ☐ NO
my own original artwork

I have read and understood the terms ☐ YES ☐ NO
of the competition

Please send your entry form and artwork to:

Overseas Submissions:
Zartarbia Ltd
Bujón 2
Calle Levante 12 P
Puerto Deportivo
29680 Estepona - Málaga
Espana

UK Submissions:
Zartarbia Ltd
'Wind In The Willows'
Donkey Lane
(off Wharf Lane)
Bourne End
Bucks SL8 5RR